RESTRAINT

COMING HOME
BOOK 3

ALLYSON LINDT

Cover Design
DAQRI BERNARDO

ACELETTE PRESS

For my eternal dragon

ONE

"I DON'T NEED THE COMPANY, THANKS. MY boyfriend gets jealous."

Despite his attempts to ignore the conversation in the booth to his right, Andrew heard every word loud and clear over the din in the steakhouse. He finished his Coke. It was nights like this he wished he still drank. Whoever was next to him had been trying to give some persistent asshole a polite brushoff for the last ten minutes. She'd said everything short of *go the fuck away*.

"If your boyfriend cared, he wouldn't make you eat dinner alone. That's why you're enjoying my company instead." That was the persistent asshole.

Andrew rolled his eyes.

His meal was over, and that meant so was the audio dinner show. It was obvious his sister was going to stand him up. As if she knew why he wanted to talk to her. He signed the bill, left a generous tip, and grabbed his credit card.

"He's working. Some people do that." Irritation crept into the woman's sweet tone.

On his way out, Andrew would ask one of the waitresses to rescue her. He wanted to get back to his hotel. It wasn't that he didn't care; no one deserved to be harassed like that. He knew how this went down if he interfered, though. Regardless of who she was, the woman would take one look at the scars on his face, and cringe away. Skin grafts had taken care of most of the damage from the third-degree burns, but the ugliness lingered.

She might try to recover and play happy to see him. She might tell him to go to hell. Either way, the rescue would be ruined.

Besides, the only reason he was in town now, rather than waiting a few weeks until Christmas was closer, was to watch the woman he used to love marry someone else. He wasn't up for another round of rejection. He pulled the hood of his sweatshirt over his face. That was the only good thing about the weather—the look wasn't out of place in this chill.

Instead of his feet moving toward the door, though, he found himself turning down the aisle and heading toward the booth that had been opposite his. He was going to regret this, but it didn't stop him.

He pasted on a gentle smile as he drew within visual range of the woman, and his brain sputtered to a halt when he saw her face. If it weren't for the blue hair that barely brushed her ears, she could be Mercy ten years ago. The first time they met. Which was ridiculous; Mercy was that much older now, same as he was. He recovered quickly, grateful his pace never faltered, and approached.

"Hey, sis. Sorry to keep you waiting." He slid into the seat across from her and braced himself for the backlash. "Snow, traffic, blah, blah, bullshit—held me up. You know how it is."

Instead of flinching or hesitating or turning away, she treated him to the brightest smile he'd ever seen. Her eyes matched the vibrant color of her hair, and everything about her expression was genuine. "Brady. I thought you weren't going to make it. So glad things worked out."

"Buddy, do you mind? We're talking." Arrogant Asshole.

She scowled. "He's my brother."

"So? You and I aren't done."

Andrew was sick of this. He stood, smile growing, and extended his hand. "So sorry to interrupt." He kept his tone cool. "I should leave you two alone."

"Thanks, man." Arrogant Asshole looked surprised, but that didn't deter him from shaking Andrew's hand.

Andrew clapped him on the other shoulder, gripped tight and moved in close. The rapid movement pressed the guy into the dividers between the booths and pinned his arm between them.

Arrogant Asshole snarled and tried to wrench free. "What the fuck?"

"It works like this." Andrew lowered his head, so his mouth was next to the guy's ear, hoping that made the dude extra uncomfortable. Andrew's voice was low and steady. "Leave the young lady alone. Tonight. Every night. Forget you ever met her."

"Fucking psychopath." Arrogant Asshole's insult drew attention from surrounding booths.

Andrew pulled back, to look him in the eye, and tightened his grip enough to hurt. He grinned, showing teeth. "How'd you know? Wanna guess which body part I take first from the guys who don't leave my baby sister alone?" His words were only meant for Arrogant Asshole's ears.

The guy wrenched free of Andrew's grip, stumbling in the process. He opened his mouth, and then snapped it shut again, before turning toward the door and all but breaking into a sprint. Once upon a time, a confrontation like this would have sent Andrew's pulse and adrenaline through the roof.

4

One of the biggest downsides to being in porn was there was at least one guy like that at every industry party. It was sad that assholeness was the norm.

Andrew braced himself to be told off and turned back to the woman with the crystal-blue eyes.

Her grin widened, and she nodded to the bench across from her. "Thank you. I didn't know how to get rid of him."

"No worries. Make sure when you leave, you ask one of the waitresses to walk you to your car." He didn't take a seat.

"You can join me. I don't bite."

He had so many pre-programmed responses to that, starting with *that's a shame* and getting filthier from there, but none seemed appropriate with her. She radiated innocence. That was disconcerting by itself. She also had to be nearly a decade younger than his twenty-eight. If she were one of his girls, she'd headline the *Barely Legal* and *Girl Next Door* pages without hesitation.

"I wasn't trying to intrude," he said.

Her smile slipped but didn't vanish. She offered her hand. "I'm Shusan."

"Andrew." Walking away now would be rude. He shook her hand and sat. Her name—minus the lisp—jarred a memory he couldn't grasp.

"Thank you again, good shir." Her words bled

into a giggle, as she gave him a mock bow. The laughter stretched on for several seconds, before she met his gaze again. Another couple of snickers slipped out. "Shorry."

"How much have you had to drink?"

"This is like my fourth Coke? They're really good here. I should shtop." She lost herself in another fit of giggles, not calming down until she hiccupped for air. She pressed her palm to her forehead. "Owie. Dizzy."

He grabbed her glass and took a sniff. No alcohol, as far as he could tell. He might be wrong, but her answer made him think she wasn't drinking. Unusual in any other state, but welcome to Utah— Mormonville USA.

If she didn't have any alcohol, that probably meant… *Shit.* A side-effect of having been a GHB addict for several years was that he knew the symptoms of the high. Odds looked good that Arrogant Asshole slipped her a roofie. "You should get home, Suzie-Q. Do you have someone you can call?"

"I drove. Why would I call someone?"

"Driving's probably not in your best interest right now. A friend? A family member?"

"Nope." She shook her head back and forth so hard, he thought it might snap off at the neck. "If my friends were free, they'd be here. Dad's out of town. Mershy's at dinner with her *fiancé.*"

His gut twisted in on itself. That explained why

6

she looked familiar. "Of all the gin joints in all the towns in all the world…" he muttered.

"What?"

"Casablanca. Mercy—your sister?"

"Does that make you *her* brother, too? How'd you know?"

Ask Mercy, and he might as well be. "I'm smarter than your average psychopath." He pulled his phone from his front pocket and dialed the familiar number. It went straight to voice mail, and he disconnected before Mercy finished asking him to leave a message. He ticked off a list of possibilities in his head. Susan was worse than drunk, and if she was lucky, she'd forget most of this in the morning. She'd also be unconscious, or as good as, in the next couple of hours.

She shouldn't be alone, so taking her back to an empty house was a bad idea. If he kept her out, he'd be the one who looked like a creeper, and he wasn't interested in spending the couple of hours in jail it would take to figure the situation out. Other towns, he'd flash a business card and hope it got him a smile and a free pass. Park City? That had a much lower probability of working out in his favor. Telling them he was the owner of the second largest internet-porn company in the world might have him rotting in a cell until his lawyer showed up in person.

"It was nice meeting you. I need to get home." She stood and stumbled.

He was on his feet in an instant, his arm around her waist. "Getting out of here is a good idea." He guided them toward the door.

Outside, tinsel trees hung from every other lamp post, lit with multi-colored lights that reflected off the snow. He'd give the town this—it was gorgeous in the winter. Maybe it wasn't so bad being here for the holidays.

He led them to his rental, grateful she didn't protest along the way. He helped her into the passenger seat.

She scowled. "'S'not my car."

"We'll grab yours later."

"'Kay."

As he walked to the driver's side, he called Mercy again. This time he was prepared to leave a message. "Miss Mercy, guess who? I need you to call me A-sap. I have a younger version of you, who needs her big sister. Did I mention A-sap? Talk soon."

"Who'd you call?" Susan asked the moment he was in the car.

"Mercy."

She pouted, crossed her arms, and sank lower in her seat. "She won't call you back. She turns off her phone when she's out with Ian and Liz."

Of course she did. In that case, they were going

back to his hotel room, and he was crossing his fingers and praying to every god and goddess who ever existed it didn't bite him in the ass.

As he headed toward his home-for-the-month, she leaned her forehead against the window. "Where are we going?" The glass muffled her question.

"My place." He probably should have explained that up front.

"Just 'cause you saved me doesn't mean you get to pop my cherry."

And she was a virgin, too. *Please, Jesus, don't let her remember any of this in the morning.* "You can keep that and everything else intact."

"Promise?"

"Cross my heart, hope to die." Out of the corner of his eye, he saw her relax in the seat, and her smile returned.

He was grateful she didn't protest when they reached their destination. Not only for his sake, but it was another reason to be relieved he interrupted the restaurant conversation when he did. If she was this pliant, he didn't want to imagine what Arrogant Asshole would have gotten away with. He *could* imagine it. Hell, he had dozens of sites devoted to the various kinks associated with the consensual version, but that didn't mean he wanted the thought.

She leaned into him on the elevator ride up. She

was soft. Warm. Smelling like sugar and vanilla. They made it down the hallway to his room, and he let her inside. She stumbled toward the bed and collapsed without another word.

Within seconds, her breathing evened out. She had to be sleeping. It gave him a better chance to study the faded T-shirt, the jeans with strategic tears along the thighs and calves, and the battered Converse. She was built like Mercy—narrow waist, subtle curves—but nothing about the way she held herself resembled her sister.

"Shtaring is creepy." She sounded drowsy.

"Sorry."

She tried to toe off her shoes and failed.

"Come on." He helped her sit up, untied the sneakers, and tugged them off.

She settled her palm on his face and used her thumb to trace the scar that ran under his eye.

He couldn't feel the contact, but he swore it burned down to his skull.

"What happened?" she asked.

"Nothing important." He helped her slide under the covers. "Old wounds. Doesn't matter."

The explanation seemed to appease her. "Okay. Thank you."

Moments later, soft snores floated from the bed. Holy fuck, it was going to be a long night. He glanced at his phone. It was only eight. Wonderful. How long until Mercy got back to him?

He settled into the chair by the bed, turned the TV on low volume, and waited. With any luck, Susan would be out of here and in a guest bed at Mercy's before she woke up and freaked out about being in a stranger's hotel room. The night was about fifty-fifty in his favor so far. He'd hold out for one more miracle.

TWO

WHEN DID A MARCHING BAND MOVE INTO SUSAN'S head? The question set off another round of stomping against her skull. She wanted to wake up, but exhaustion weighed down everything, including her eyelids. Processing her thoughts felt like dragging them through molasses.

She heard noises in the background. A voice? It sounded like half a conversation.

Was that her name?

"Don't force it." The voice was distant. And male. And sexy, in a confident, careless kind of way. And unfamiliar. "Take it easy." And right next to her, instead of miles away.

As each realization clicked, her panic grew, until the marching band was joined by a thunderstorm. She summoned her strength, to force her eyes open. Realization slammed into her sluggish brain. This wasn't her room. She didn't know whose it was, but those were ugly curtains.

"It takes time to shake the fog." The guy sitting in the chair next to the bed, studying her, was so completely a stranger, it wasn't funny.

Adrenaline slammed through her veins, kicking up the bedlam in her skull. She jolted upright and scooted away until her back hit the wall. Her heart hammered against her ribs. "Who the hell are you?"

"Andrew. You don't remember." He sounded as if he expected it.

She dug through the mire, searching for snippets of the familiar. There was a guy in the steakhouse. Irritating. Wouldn't go the heck away. It wasn't this dude, though. "No." The answer came out more timid than she intended. Why weren't the memories there?

His smile was sympathetic. The right corner of his mouth didn't pull up all the way; it collided with a scar running from his ear down to his jaw. He was kind of cute. And a little terrifying, given she didn't know who he was. "Best guess? GHB. Rohypnol. A drug along those lines. And I'm guessing you didn't take it willingly."

"Like, date-rape drugs?" Her stomach churned, and acid surged into her throat. "What did you do to me?" Better question—how was she going to get out of here?

He held up his hands and leaned away. "Whoa. Not me. Some douchenut who was bugging you."

"Then why am I here with you?" Slivers of the evening struggled to surface, and they matched his story, but she didn't trust them. Not when she couldn't think straight.

"You sounded like you needed a hand, so I stepped in. We told him I was your brother."

"And then you brought me to a hotel? Is this Deer Valley?" At least, if he'd assaulted her, he chose one of the most expensive resorts around. How... *classy*? She was still clothed. Her shoes were missing, but everything else was intact. And no pain *down there*. Not that she had any idea what that would feel like. None of this made sense.

"It's The Chateaux. I didn't want anyone making the assumptions you're making before I could call your sister and have her come get you."

Maybe this was a hidden-camera show. Or The Twilight Zone. Or the most screwed up dream she'd had in ever. "What makes you think I have a sister?"

"Because she talks about you. Susan Rice. You're eight years younger. Only sibling she has who likes her."

"Everyone knows that. Half the town is familiar with our family drama."

He chuckled.

"What?" Frustration joined the churning inside.

"Mercy told me you were stubborn. You're a lot

like her. I don't know how you're thinking through the drugs. Low dosage, I suppose."

"What?"

"Mercy. Told. Me—"

"You didn't call her *Melissa*." Susan was coming further out of the fog, and her logic believed this man. *Andrew*. His name sounded familiar. Did he give it to her earlier?

He raised his left brow. She wasn't sure if the single raise was on purpose, or because of the scarring. "She hates that name," he said.

"So you might know her. Maybe."

"You were a lot more trusting in the steakhouse. Good drugs. If it makes you feel better, you can walk out the door right now. I promise I won't stop you. You can take the elevator down to the front desk and call the police and Mercy. She'll vouch for me. Fuck." He lifted his butt off the chair, reached into his pocket, pulled out a wallet and a phone, and tossed both on the bed. They landed near her without a sound. "You can call from here if you want, and see I am who I say I am."

She opened the leather wallet, alternating her gaze between him and it. His driver's license was from Atlanta and said he was Andrew Newton. She definitely knew that name. Why? The logo on his business cards was a silhouette of a curvy woman with horns and a halo. The company name was *Smut Central*. That was why he was familiar. Sure enough, his title was *CEO and Lord High God of Smut.* If he was lying about his identity, it was the most elaborate setup ever.

"Mercy didn't answer when you tried to get a hold of her," she said.

"Not the first time. You told me she turns off her phone."

"She does." Why couldn't Susan remember any of that?

"I left her a message. Told her I met some groupie, who loves my work, in a bar, and we came back here and fucked like bunnies, and now you need a ride."

Her face heated to scorching. "You didn't."

"No. I told her to call me A-sap. I won't share details unless you want help filling in the blanks. She got back to me right before you woke up. She'll be here in about"—he glanced at the clock—"five minutes."

"Oh." Susan wasn't sure what else to say. Her head pounded. She desperately wanted to curl up and go to sleep. Things barely made sense, despite the explanation. Every time she tried to grasp a thought—a flash from earlier tonight—it slipped away. Sometimes she caught the tail, but others vanished in a *poof.* "Thank you."

He waved a hand, and turned his gaze away. "Yeah. If you're okay, Ima watch TV till Mercy gets here."

She nodded, though he wasn't looking at her anymore. With her heart rate returning to normal and the mental haze slowly lifting, it sank in how much her head hurt. Especially when she tried to wrap it around the situation. What would have happened if he hadn't been there? Didn't know Mercy? Hadn't cared one way or another? Would Susan be waking up with far fewer clothes, in a not-so-kind stranger's bed?

Her gut lurched. Bile surged into her throat. She stumbled from the bed, and her legs threatened to give out. She bolted for the bathroom. She kicked the door shut behind her and reached the toilet, before the contents of her stomach evicted themselves. The heaves continued after there was nothing left to vomit, and she knelt in front of the porcelain, hating that she had the extra-hot salsa on her nacho burger. The thought made her want to hurl again.

Tears and sweat streamed down her cheeks. She was so stupid to let this happen. A nagging voice reminded her it wasn't her fault, but she knew better. Always be alert.

Someone knocked nearby, and seconds later, she heard the squeak of hinges. Then Mercy's voice. She and Andrew spoke in hushed tones, so Susan couldn't make out the words.

Susan waited until she was sure she wouldn't puke again, then extracted herself from where she knelt on the floor.

"You alive in there?" Andrew's question carried through the bathroom door.

"Yeah." The word rasped out of her throat. She looked in the mirror. Red-rimmed eyes stared back, studying blotchy cheeks and swollen lips. *Gah*. She was a wreck. She splashed cold water on her face. Now she was a drowned wreck, but her skin was cooler.

When someone pushed into the room, she whirled, startled. Andrew didn't so much as twitch at her appearance. He held out two cups. "Water. Don't swallow it; rinse your mouth out. Mouthwash. You know how that works. When the nasty vomit taste is gone, drink some water. Tiny sips. No gulping."

Mercy moved around him—the most welcome sight Susan had seen all night. She rubbed Susan's back. "You okay?"

"No." More tears threatened, and Susan swallowed them back. She turned away, cups in hand, and followed Andrew's instructions, not trusting herself to speak. The mouthwash burned, and she fought her gag reflex. It was pathetic. She didn't care.

"I'll give you a few minutes to wash up. Come out when you're ready," Mercy said.

Susan closed her eyes and focused on calming down. Knowing security sat outside the door helped. When she was ready, she headed back into the main room.

Mercy sat next to Andrew on the bed, their heads bowed together as they talked in hushed voices. They looked comfortable, as if this was how they spent every free night. According to Mercy's stories, they had, when they were younger. The two toured a lot of South America and Europe together, in their late teens and early twenties. It was how they met.

A pang of envy knocked behind Susan's ribs. For Mercy's experiences. That she had this close friend here and an amazing fiancé at home.

Andrew stood and grabbed Susan's Converse from the floor next to him. He handed them over with a sympathetic smile.

She was grateful he didn't say anything, because she didn't have a lot of brainpower for talking; she used most of it doing up the laces on her shoes.

Mercy moved to stand next to Andrew. She squeezed his hand. "Thank you. See you Monday?"

"I'll be there." He met Susan's gaze. "Take care of yourself, Suzie-Q."

The nickname made her cringe, but a portion of her liked the quirk of his mouth when he said it. She returned the smile.

Moments later, she dropped into the passenger seat of Mercy's battered Honda. The worn leather was already warm from the heater. With comfort around her, reality threatened to overwhelm Susan again, reminding her how bad things almost got, and she shuddered. "Can I stay with you guys tonight?" She managed to talk without her voice cracking.

"Of course. Don't want to face Dad?"

Susan frowned at the implication. She didn't like the nudge that, while Mercy and Dad were on speaking terms after years of being out of each other's lives, there wasn't any trust between them. The thought gave Susan a new focus, and she was grateful for that. "He's in Seattle."

"Oh. You know you're always welcome. Do you want to tell me what happened?" Mercy rested a hand on Susan's knee.

"Not yet. I need time." Susan saw Mercy's brow furrow. "Nothing bad. Not *that* bad. But I need to process." She had no idea how, but she'd figure it out. "Thank you for coming to get me at— *Holy wow.* Is it really three in the morning?"

"Of course. You'll be more careful next time, won't you?" Mercy clamped her jaw shut and frowned. "I didn't mean it like that. You shouldn't have to be. Whatever happened wasn't your fault."

"I know." Susan didn't believe it, though, and her sister's slip added to the doubt. When they got inside Mercy and Ian's house, Susan mumbled *good-night* and stumbled off to her part-time room.

She fell into bed without taking off her clothes.

The soft quilt and feather pillow hugged her, and the scent of fabric softener squeezed with comfort. For a moment, her head felt like it might roll away, but equilibrium returned quickly. She expected to sleep for ages, based on the exhaustion raking her bones.

She rolled onto her side and watched the shadows warp and twist across the textured wall and bleed into the burgundy accent. Snippets of the evening popped in and out of her mind, but not the ones she expected. Instead of terrifying her, the conversations with Andrew kept her company; his compassion, irritation, and sense of humor.

She flopped onto her back and studied the vaulted ceiling, trying to make out where the apex vanished in the shadows. As night gave way to the gray of the oncoming morning, she couldn't get the thoughts of Andrew out of her head. Her knight in shining armor was her sister's porn-friend. The guy who helped Mercy shed her inhibitions and discover what life was really about when she was Susan's age.

It wasn't the first time Susan wished she could live that experience without having to surrender her friends and family—she could never abandon this life without caring, the way Mercy had—but the thought hit harder and lingered longer tonight. It would be nice to find a friend like Andrew, without having to go to South America to do so.

THREE

Susan felt a lot better than last night, after sleeping off whatever drugs might have been in her system.

Waking up in a house where she wouldn't get a sigh when she refused to accompany her father to church. A long, hot shower. Outside, the sun bounced off the snow, bright and warm. Today would be a good day.

Her phone said it was close to eleven. Later than she normally got started, but it meant Mercy should be up.

Susan wandered downstairs. The white a Christmas tree, covered in gold and cream ornaments, winked at her through the living room doorway. She headed toward the murmur of voices. The open dining room flowed into the kitchen, divided up by a breakfast bar, then continuing into polished walnut, granite counters, and stainless steel. Mercy stood near the stove with Ian behind her, arms around her waist. Their backs were to Susan. He nuzzled Mercy's neck, and she laughed and leaned into him.

Such a perfect couple. Susan wanted to be half of that kind of adoration someday, but that didn't mean she wanted to watch them grope each other. She cleared her throat. And then again.

Mercy whirled, grinning. "Hey. You sleep okay?"

"Once I finally passed out, it was good." Susan adored having Mercy back in her life. She was so young when her sister left. And Mercy saw and experienced so much. Susan wished it hadn't been at the cost of family, but now they were back together. Besides, Ian was nice. The house had a happy presence to it.

Ian kissed Mercy on the cheek. "Give me ten, and we'll go." He squeezed Susan's arm. "Brunch?"

"Absolutely," Susan said. Her phone rang.

Mercy frowned. "I'm sorry last night it took me so long…"

"Don't worry about it." Susan ignored the pang of hurt at the reminder. "I have to take this." She clicked *Answer* and turned to pace toward the living room. "This is Susan Rice."

"Susan, it's Grace, with Ballet West."

Susan's heart dropped into her stomach, and she swallowed back the surge of nervousness. "It's great to hear from you." She'd auditioned with the group for the last four years, with no luck. But this would be her year. She knew it.

"Same." A hint of strain ran through the woman's voice. "Listen, I'm sorry to bother you on a Sunday." She laughed, but cut it off abruptly. "We don't normally call back at all, in cases like this, but I wanted to talk to you."

Susan ran the words through every second-guess filter in her brain. She wanted this job. Had prayed to make it through this audition. It wasn't a big part, but if she performed well for their next season, she could move into larger roles in future years. It would also look fantastic on her resume, when she finished college and started teaching. It should be a stepping stone to instructing a high school drill team. She wanted this so bad she could taste it. "It's not a problem. What can I do for you?"

"Ms. Rice, you're very talented. It's been years since I've seen such technically skilled performance."

The words didn't boost her spirits the way they should. "Thank you."

"But this kind of performance requires a stage presence, which—to be direct—you're lacking. This is a difficult thing to explain, but you don't have a gift for playing to the audience."

Susan swallowed a whimper. It wasn't the first time she'd heard feedback like this. It kept her out of all but the one-off background dancer gigs, where she was cast to the back row. She'd never figured out what to do with the information. "Is there some way I can learn?" The question slipped out before she could stop it, carried on a pleading she wanted to hide. "I know you don't have time. But if you could recommend someone—" She snapped her jaw shut before she resorted to flat-out begging.

"I'm sorry, Ms. Rice. It's not that easy. The kind of presence you're lacking isn't the kind of thing one normally learns. The best advice I have for you is to do more in front of audiences. Do it until it's as natural as dancing when no one's watching. Come back during group try-outs in January. We might have an opening then, and you can see about observing from the background."

"Of course. Thank you."

"And Ms. Rice? You only have a few more years left. I'd love to see a talent like yours perform with us before you pass your peak."

"Me too." Susan failed to keep the bitterness from her voice. "Enjoy your Sunday." She disconnected and dropped her cell phone onto the couch, before sinking down next to it. The fire crackled in the hearth, and the snap of a log blended with her mood. Dang it.

"Everything all right?"

Mercy's question startled her, and Susan shifted

to see her standing in the doorway. "Fine. Good. Status quo. Didn't get the Ballet West thing. No big deal."

"I'm sorry. I know how much you wanted that."

Susan wasn't in the mood for pity or sympathy or anything obligatory. She had her fill of that last night. "It's fine. But I'm not up for brunch. Can you give me a lift back to my car?"

Sympathy bled into Mercy's smile. "Of course. You know where to find me if you want to talk."

"I do." Susan didn't want to talk. Wasn't in the mood to get another lecture on living her dreams and pushing to achieve. What the heck did Mercy think she was *trying* to do? Susan buried the acrid thought. She needed a little time to work through this.

ANDREW PARKED in the lot of the four-story building near the freeway. He'd been to the Rowe and Thompson offices a couple times, since Mercy and Ian merged their advertising firms. Andrew was Mercy's oldest client, but the visits were as much social as business. And they gave him a chance to visit his sister and nephew, while he was in the state.

Despite his past with Mercy, he was surprised she had room in her schedule for him, what with her getting married next weekend and all. When he asked her about the timing, she said she wasn't going to stop working because one of the biggest days of her life was coming up—besides, this was a nice distraction from the insanity, and she had new campaign metrics and concepts to go over with him.

He couldn't say *no* to that. Her work helped make him what he was, and she never disappointed. They had a friend, Justin, who had turned a Silicon Valley startup, based on a rewards program, into something bigger. More artificial-intelligence-like. R&T had invited some of their clients to beta-test demographic information, and Smut Central was first on the list.

Andrew strolled into the office and pasted on his biggest smile for the girl at Reception. "Hey, Candy Cane. Miss Mercy is expecting me."

The woman's name was Mindy, but she had a preference for painting her nails red with white tips. She returned his grin, pressed a few buttons on her phone, and seconds later said, "Mr. Newton is here." She looked back at Andrew. "She says ten minutes."

Of course she did. Mercy was a lot of things he adored, including *just let me finish this up, and I'll be right with you.*

He walked the short lobby while he waited. Normally he'd make small talk with Mindy, but he'd been on edge since Saturday night. A thought nagged him, and he couldn't place it. Music drifted toward him. Rock, but played by a string quartet. Apocolyptica. It came from the in-house photography studio. He wandered toward the sound, and cracked the door open, to peek in.

The screens and lights sat in the corners of the room, as they usually did when no filming was being done, leaving a wide expanse of concrete. That wasn't what stalled his thoughts. Susan was in the middle of the open space, dancing. It was a stunning combination of ballet and more modern moves, and she flowed with every note and beat. Watching her chased away his tension about work and the strange funk that taunted him. It didn't hurt that her bodysuit and tights clung to every inch of her body, but it was her grace that held him captive.

When the music stopped, she dropped to one knee, shoulders heaving, chin on her chest.

He clapped.

She shot to her feet and whirled, eyes wide. "No one's supposed to come in here when there's music playing." Pink flushed her cheeks.

"I'm not anyone. And you're fucking talented."

Her blush grew. "You don't have to say that, to be nice."

"You're right; I don't. I mean it. You've been doing this all your life?"

She bit her bottom lip. "It feels like it, sometimes."

Mercy interrupted. "Sorry to keep you waiting."

"Don't say it unless you mean it." Andrew kept the teasing in his voice but didn't face her. It was harder than he expected, to pull his gaze from the elegant form in the center of the room.

Mercy sighed, but a hint of amusement ran through the sound. "She's not on the menu."

When he thought Susan couldn't turn any redder, she proved him wrong.

He finally turned away. "You know me. Hold the cherries on the dessert," Andrew said. Taking someone's virginity was as lucrative a fetish as anything in his business, but it wasn't one of his fantasies. He lived that dream when he was younger.

Mercy rolled her eyes and nodded toward the offices. "Come on. I think you're going to like what we came up with."

He glanced over his shoulder. "See you around Suzie-Q."

"I hope so." Her smile was the most genuine thing he'd seen all day. His imagination did him the favor of showing him what she'd look like on her knees, mouth wrapped around his cock. Moans vibrating against the head. Susan sliding her fingers between her legs to press through spandex and make herself come.

That was distracting. He shook the thought away and followed Mercy.

Her office was as big as her entire rented space

had been before the merger. She never seemed to mind the upgrade from faded carpet and metal cabinets to the leather and wood of this place.

"I know I don't have to ask this, but humor me, because I'm going to anyway." She settled into her chair, and he took the seat across from her.

"Anything for you."

"Stay away from Susan?"

He hadn't expected that. His shock slipped out before he could stop it. "She's an adult. Isn't that her call to make? She *is* an adult, isn't she?"

"She's twenty-one."

"Legal and then some. Hell, she's nearly a cougar. What makes you think I'm looking?"

"Please." Mercy gave a short laugh. "I practically heard you get a hard-on, watching her."

Sometimes being predictable sucked. "Guilty as charged. Does your fiancé know you've got an obsession with how my dick spends its time?"

"He watches me finger myself to the pictures every night."

He was grateful she was making jokes. "I knew he had to have at least one redeemable trait for you to love him," he said.

"I'm serious about Susan."

"So am I." He was tired of this conversation. It was a reasonable request, but he didn't like that Mercy kept pushing it. "I'm not in the market to corrupt someone. If she's not wicked on her own, let a different pervert pave the path. I suffered enough watching you and me break. But I'll keep my distance. Cross my heart, hope to die."

When she winced, he recognized his poor choice of words. It sank heavy in his chest. "That's not what I meant."

"I get that. The phrasing hit me hard is all. Old scars. Not as deep as yours, but there."

He didn't have a reply for that. He understood exactly what she meant and wasn't interested in delving into that part of their past. "Now that the dirty work is out of the way"—he forced the cheer into his tone—"show me the goods, Miss Mercy."

FOUR

Susan shouldered her duffel bag and headed toward the exit of the Rowe and Thompson offices. No one else was in, this time of morning. Heck, even the sun was barely peeking its head over the mountains. She couldn't ignore the trace of disappointment that she had to work today. Part of her hoped, if she came in later—around nine or ten—she'd *accidentally* run into Andrew, like she had yesterday. Mercy set up a temporary office for him while he was in town, so he could work closely with her staff. Susan wasn't sure what it was about him that fascinated her, but she wanted more time with him, to figure it out.

She pushed out the front door. When she collided with someone, it sent her stumbling back a few steps.

"Watch yourself," the man said.

Andrew.

He rested his hands on her shoulders and steadied her. "Lost in thought, Suzie-Q?"

"I guess so." She met his gaze. He had stunning brown eyes. The kind of dark that was almost black and easy to drown in. She wasn't going to be flustered, the way she was yesterday. He'd caught her off-guard, watching her dance, but this time she had her wits about her. Third impressions counted for something, didn't they? "You're in early." And that was less than brilliant.

"Yet you're already leaving." The way he looked her over, lingering on her hips and breasts, sent goosebumps racing across her skin.

It made her wish she wore clothing more fitted than yoga pants and a T-shirt. "I have to get to work, but I wanted to get some practice time in before."

"There has to be a better place for you to practice than a photography room."

"The studio I study at is in the valley." Too long a drive for a morning session. There was room at home, but her dad didn't understand why she pursued such a childish dream. She was lucky Ian let her use this place. It was quiet and private.

"Makes sense." Andrew leaned against the side of the building, not looking like he was in a hurry to be anywhere. "Mercy says you're really talented.

Professional quality. What are the odds you can hook me up with tickets, while I'm in town?"

Maybe he was being polite, but his interest flooded her with heat—some of it embarrassment-related. "I… uh… wouldn't hold your breath."

"No? I promise I can pretend to be classy when the occasion calls for it."

"It's not that." She shifted her weight from one foot to the other. "I haven't had any luck getting parts."

"*What?* I saw you yesterday. You're brilliant."

She resisted the urge to ask him how much he knew about dancing. To the untrained eye, a lot of people looked good. That didn't mean they were. "I don't quite make the cut. I don't have *stage presence*, whatever that means." She regretted the confession the moment it slipped out. She braced herself for the same type of *you'll get it next time* or *you need to try harder* that most people gave her.

"I get that." His answer caught her off guard. "I see it with actors sometimes. Brilliant when no one's watching, but as soon as they know the cameras are rolling, all the boom goes out of the bang."

Her brain skipped ahead several steps and kindly pointed out he was talking about porn. *Thanks for that, mind.* "But isn't everyone that way?" She shouldn't have asked that. Not that she was embarrassed to talk about sex; she was inexperienced, but not uptight. That didn't mean she wanted him to know *how* inexperienced.

"What way?"

"Good at sex when the cameras aren't rolling?" What the heck was wrong with her this morning? This was the opposite of sounding less-than-naïve.

He raised his brow, amusement tugging up one side of his mouth. "You'll be happier if you believe that."

Great. Now he thought she was dim, too. "Don't condescend to me. I know better. I don't understand why there's a difference between in front of the camera and behind."

"You just told me you did. It's the same as you and dancing. I saw you yesterday. When you don't know anyone's watching, you flow like water. I'd guess you freeze up on stage."

"That's ridiculous. I've been doing things like public speaking since I was a kid."

He shook his head. "Talking in church is different."

"That's not—" She snapped her jaw shut and took a few seconds to process her thoughts before speaking. "So... you've got someone who wants to do *movies*, but they can't do it when people are watching. Do you tell them the cameras aren't on, and then trick them? Or do they find different work?"

"There are ways around it. Learned hang-ups can be unlearned."

"How?" No one had given her information about this before. Sympathy, reassurance, false hope—yes. But not an actual solution.

"It's not a simple thing. I can't hand you a self-help brochure."

Her optimism evaporated. "Oh." Her phone chimed, and she grabbed it. "Crap. I'm late to work. I'll see you around?"

"Count on it."

She couldn't fight her smile as she headed toward her car. It was nice to have a conversation with someone who didn't treat her like a child. Or try to shelter her. Or tell her she was going to hell for anything but chaste thoughts. On top of that, he made her think she might be able to fix whatever was holding her back in auditions. Next step was getting the details out of him.

ANDREW SETTLED into the office that would be his temporary business-home until Christmas, but his mind wasn't on work. Susan fascinated him. She was a unique combination of innocent, bold, and curious. He meant what he told Mercy, though; he wasn't in the market to teach someone how to be wicked. As long as he kept that in mind, he'd be fine when Susan was around. She was another girl, nothing more.

His cell phone rang, jarring him back to the present. When he saw Kandace's name on the caller ID, he answered without hesitation. "Hey, sis."

"Is now a good time?"

"Sure. Everything okay?" His relationship with his sister was complicated when it came to her son, Lucas. Kandace was ten years older than Andrew. When he was eighteen, he decided backpacking around the world was the best way to experience life. It was how he met Mercy.

He was in South America when he found out he had a son. His high school girlfriend dropped the boy on Kandace's porch only sticking around long enough to sign the adoption papers. Kandace took custody of Lucas months before she could track Andrew down to tell him. Andrew and Kandace agreed she was a more stable force for the baby, and he sent support home, while she raised Lucas as her own.

Andrew hated that he couldn't be more a part of Lucas's life, but over the last year, as he spent more time here for business, his regret that his role was relegated to *uncle* grew.

"Fine. Good. Everything's great. I'm sorry for standing you up on Saturday." An underlying current of stress ran through Kandace's voice.

When Andrew had asked for a bit of her time

while he was in town, she'd hesitated, which she'd never done before, and that put him on edge. "You know I love the small talk, but I'm gonna cut you off. What happened?" he said.

"Lucas's gay."

Andrew shrugged, though no one was there to see him. "All right. Do you want me to give him *the talk*? Is ten too young for that? Are they ever too young?"

"Could you take things seriously for two minutes?"

Her irritation caught him off guard. "I'm being serious. It's not a big deal."

"You're not giving him *the talk*. And it is a big deal."

"So give him a big hug, tell him you love him regardless, and point him toward the internet. Or let me take him for the day. Sit down with him. Explain the birds and the bees and who his real father is." He hadn't meant to slip that in until he had a chance to build up to it, but he was glad it was out there.

"Stop." Her word cut over the line. "He didn't come out to me. Perhaps it's not that binary. I don't know. The problem is bigger than that. One of the sisters at school caught him kissing a male classmate."

And rapped him on the knuckles with a ruler? Andrew swallowed the question but didn't miss how she ignored his statement about telling Lucas the truth. "And?"

"And she and the school are recommending conversion therapy."

"*What?*" He wasn't letting a holier-than-thou zealot in a penguin suit brainwash his kid into believing being attracted to anything besides the opposite sex was evil. "There's a reason states are making that illegal. There's no fucking way, in this world or the next—"

"And Lucas wants to do it."

A chill raced through Andrew, and he shuddered involuntarily. "No. Why? This is why you shouldn't have sent him to Catholic school." It was also another reason Andrew wanted to bring the boy back into his life. The private schools were good for Lucas's education, but he needed a different influence, to offset the indoctrination.

Andrew was tempted to step in and just tell Lucas the truth. Take him away from this. But Kandace held a pretty big anvil over Andrew's head —as Lucas's legal guardian, she had the power to take him out of Andrew's life completely. He didn't think she'd actually do something that severe, but this was a topic he wasn't willing to call *bluff* on.

"You wanted him to have the best education in the state," she said.

Like Andrew needed the reminder. "I know."

"And the only reason I'm telling you what's

going on is because you sign the checks to the school." Her tone grew cold.

"Why does he want to do this?"

"He says they're right. He thinks evil things about other boys, and he hates himself for it."

Jesus. "I'll come down tonight for dinner, and we'll figure out what to do next."

"We won't be home until Sunday. And you're not hearing me. You can come visit, but you don't get a say in how things go down. I agree with you—letting him do this is dangerous and stupid—but I'll figure out what happens next."

"Then why loop me in?" Not that he was complaining. He needed to figure out how to stop this. "There's an easy answer. I'll sit down, we'll talk about where he comes from, and I'll remind him porn pays the bills and tell him that, if he's going to hell, he should enjoy the ride." Turned out he was in the mood to push the parenthood issue.

"You're usually better at picking up on my *no*'s. I don't want you to tell him the truth. He barely knows you. Don't walk your ass in here and change that for your own ego. He's doing fine the way things are. Come down, visit, be a strong *uncle* figure, and remind him it's okay to be him."

Okay for Lucas, but not Andrew apparently. A logical part of him agreed with his sister, coercing him to back down. Lucas had a stable life, believing the woman who raised him was his mother and not getting caught up in the insanity that was Andrew's world. The last thing Andrew wanted was to make Lucas miserable. "I'll drop by early next week. Hang out with him. *Casually and unobtrusively* remind him manly men can like men, and it'll be fine."

Her sigh echoed in his ear. "Thank you."

"I want what's best for him," Andrew said.

"We'll see you Monday." She disconnected.

He tossed his phone aside and dropped his face into his hands. *Conversion therapy. Fuck.*

FIVE

Andrew looked over the last of the sample creative Mercy laid on the desk between them. "You can get away with this in print now?" he said. Strategic text, blurs, and graphics covered nipples and pussy but not much else. The woman in the picture looked like she was on the edge of the ultimate orgasm.

"I've run the basics by the sales team at that men's magazine you like. They say there's no guy and there are no *naughty bits* showing, so it's acceptable. You've seen their articles. This is tame."

She had a point.

"I'm sold. Run with it." While he spoke, her attention drifted to something behind him. He glanced over his shoulder, but her office door was closed, and he didn't see anything through the windows on either side. "What's up?"

"I'm meeting Susan for lunch, and she's pacing out there in the hallway."

The name sent a spike through Andrew, teasing his thoughts and gliding over his skin. He wasn't used to this kind of reaction to something as simple as the possibility of seeing someone. "We can wrap things up and pick up later if needed. No reason to keep her waiting." He stood before Mercy could argue, and opened the door. "We're almost done," he said to Susan.

The conversation about him keeping his distance lingered in the back of his mind, but Mercy was simply looking out for her younger sister. Since Andrew didn't plan on hitting on Susan, he didn't have to cut off contact with her. Besides, this wasn't about him; they were the ones meeting up.

Susan hesitated in the doorway. "I don't want to interrupt."

"You're not." Andrew nodded at an empty seat. He swore he heard a low growl behind him, but when he looked at Mercy, she smiled.

Susan glanced at the artwork on the desk, then did a double-take. She tilted her head to one side and studied it more closely. "Is that supposed to be erotic?"

"It is." Mercy sounded amused.

"But it's so… I mean… I don't understand how that's physically possible."

Andrew leaned back, one ankle on the other

knee. "When a girl meet's a guy who's really well hung—"

"That's not what I mean." Susan pursed her lips, still staring at the image. "That pose looks really painful, and this is coming from someone who can put her foot behind her head."

Andrew swallowed a groan at the image Susan's admission provoked, and tried to ignore Mercy's glare. He'd promised not to corrupt Susan, but there was no reason he couldn't have a little fun. "Sometimes pain is the point."

Susan's cheeks turned a charming shade of dark pink. "I'm not talking about a slap to the behind or a little hair pulling. This is an *I've got a cramp, and if I don't walk it off soon, I won't be walking for days* kind of agony. I'm sure camera angle is important for that money shot, but at least make it plausible."

This discussion shouldn't be turning him on the way it was. "I'll make a note to tell the photographer. Would you like to put your experienced eye on the rest of this campaign creative?"

Susan bit her bottom lip. Everything from her curious gaze to her flush to her quickened breathing said she was turned on. Fuck, if Andrew wasn't tempted to push a little harder, to see how far things could go.

"You know what?" Irritation edged Mercy's voice. "We're almost done here. Susan, do you want to wait in the lobby, and I'll be right out?"

"Sure." Susan gave Andrew one last glance, then left.

Mercy twisted a lock of hair around her finger hard enough it pulled her scalp. "Please?"

She was referring to her request to keep his distance from Susan. "We were talking. You're not really policing her friends, are you?"

"You're asking her to look at porn with you."

"*Creative.* Nothing worse than what you and I look at."

"Except I know exactly what you look and sound like when you're trying to get laid."

Ridiculous. He didn't want to fuck Susan—just to see what kind of buttons she had. Though now that the image was there... "You're acting like you don't trust me," he said.

"I'm not stupid enough to forget the past."

It was a simple phrase, but it sliced deep, and Andrew frowned. "You're not seriously talking about something that happened seven years ago."

"I am."

He and Mercy dated, briefly, under the condition they had an option relationship. The first time he explored the *see other people* aspect of things, she decided she didn't like the arrangement. It almost destroyed their friendship, but he thought they got over that back then. "I'm having fun with her. Nothing else. Even if I were interested in more, I'd be as honest with her as I was with you.

"I'm asking. I'm begging. I'm appealing to you as a friend." Mercy held his gaze. "I get that I don't have a say in who she hangs out with. She's a big girl; she can make up her own mind. But *please* don't do to her what you did to me."

Andrew wanted to laugh the whole thing off. Remind Mercy he didn't do anything to her she didn't agree to. Give any number of brush-offs. But her request dragged back painful memories. When she severed ties with him all those years ago, what followed was some dark shit. Not just because he lost her friendship, but that was part of it. He didn't want to go back to that, and he wasn't interested in destroying the bond they shared. "I promise. I'll be on my best behavior around Susan. Even better, I'll behave like Ian would."

Mercy's lips twitched in a half smile. "Bullshit. You're not capable."

"Maybe not, but I'll try."

"Thank you." She gathered up the artwork they'd been discussing and shoved it in a folder. "Talk to you this afternoon."

SIX

Andrew swept his gaze over the room. Mercy and Ian's wedding reception was like a junior-high dance, with her friends from her travels on one side of the room, and his from work and college on the other.

Andrew was only a little surprised that Mercy's father didn't walk her down the aisle. Despite Dean Rice making amends, her relationship with him was strained. Andrew steered clear of the older man. They met once, at a client summit for R&T. Dean made no secret of the fact he didn't like Andrew's work—and by extension Andrew—and thought he was to blame for Mercy's founding her advertising agency on something as revolting as selling porn.

As much as Andrew thought most marriages were bullshit scams for both bride and groom, the ceremony had been beautiful. Mercy was gorgeous in an off-the-shoulder gown with a hand-beaded train, and Ian watched her walk down the aisle with what could only be described as pure, open adoration.

Now the happy couple stood with their wedding party, greeting guests and wearing pasted-on smiles. If they could bear their way through an entire night of this, Andrew could wait in line to wish them well.

The handshake he exchanged with Ian was stiff. "Congratulations," Andrew said.

"Thank you."

And that was that. Andrew didn't have a problem with the guy per se, but Ian struck him as lacking in the ever-so-important sense-of-humor and chilling-the-fuck-out departments.

Mercy was next. Andrew kissed her on the cheek. "You look stunning."

"Thank you. For everything. Ever." She pulled him into a hug and squeezed.

"Always." He swallowed past the lump in his throat. The gratitude went both ways. He wouldn't be here—among the living—if it weren't for her.

He repeated the ritual with Liz, minus the choked-up feeling. Unlike her brother, Liz seemed to know how to enjoy the world.

When he reached Susan, his brain froze. A ridiculous reaction. It wasn't as though he'd spent the week avoiding her for reasons he couldn't explain. He greeted her the same way he had the other women. A kiss on the cheek and a brief, bible-between-them, chaste hug. It didn't stop the familiar scent of sugar and vanilla from drilling into his head and taunting him. She even *smelled* like innocence and fresh baked cookies.

When he dipped his head close, she whispered, "Can we talk?"

"No." His promise to Mercy echoed in his head. Talking to Susan wasn't a bad idea by itself, but something about the request set off warning bells in his head.

He pulled away in time to see a scowl ghost in before her smile evicted it. She turned to the person behind him without another glance in Andrew's direction.

She was good. How many events like this had she been marched through in her life?

He stowed the question, but it wasn't as easy to get her request out of his head. Or rather, his reaction. What was it about her that both captivated him and set off his every warning bell—besides Mercy's simple and reasonable request?

He couldn't stop thinking about Susan, though, and every few minutes, his gaze drifted back to her. Her naïveté seemed genuine, and her attempts to hide it were standard, but there was more to it—to her—and he couldn't name what that was.

He shoved aside the thought and worked his way through catching up with friends he and Mercy met while travelling. He caught the attention of Justin Conroy and approached him.

"Hey, old man." Andrew clapped him on the shoulder.

Justin shook his head. He was only four years older, but when in their early twenties, that had seemed like centuries. "Whatever. Mercy know you've got designs on her little sister?"

"It's not like that." Was Andrew that obvious?

"Long story, right? You need time to polish it before you share?" From his tailored suit, down to the pewter cufflinks, Justin looked like he belonged on Ian's side of the dance floor. It was a good mask. The man was a wicked-brilliant programmer, who was more comfortable talking movie trivia than socializing. The tattoos hidden under his sleeves were the result of years of work, done by various artists, in every country he visited. Andrew and Mercy had been there for some of them.

"Never let Mercy think there's any kind of story. There's not. Nothing there."

Justin squinted and studied him. "I'm sorry— what? I think I'm talking to the wrong guy."

"You're funny. Barrel of monkeys." Andrew fought the desire to glance back at Susan. No reason to make this worse. "Mercy hooked me up with your beta earlier this week. You collected all that in five years?"

"I've got a good team."

A movement caught Andrew's attention, and he turned in time to see Susan vanish out a side door.

"And… I've lost you." Justin sounded amused.

Andrew turned back to the conversation. "Still here. Bummed your fiancée couldn't make it. Lia, isn't it? I wanted to see what kind of woman you suckered into marrying you."

Justin laughed. "The kind who likes money. Seriously, though, she's amazing." His dopey in-love look wasn't quite as bright as Mercy's, but it shone. "Next time you're in San Jose, we'll do dinner. It's even on me if you don't make it down until the wedding."

Andrew swapped a few more inanities with him, but Justin was fidgeting. They parted ways. The desire to mingle with the rest of the crowd faded, and Andrew headed outside.

The December cold bit into his face when he stepped into the evening. It was a nice change from the hot air blowing inside. The salt on the sidewalk crunched beneath his shoes, sounding louder than it should in the still night. He wandered the frozen path, past iced-over bushes and pine trees.

Susan stood near a balcony overlooking the mountainside. She didn't look up as he approached, but when he reached her, she spun in the other direction and brushed past him. "I'll leave you alone."

He grabbed her arm harder than he intended,

and she let out a half-groan, half-hiss. It wasn't an irritated noise. She liked it? He dropped his hand away quickly. "You wanted to talk?"

"Don't worry about it." Her tone was dismissive. "You'll enjoy your evening more if you find someone who doesn't rattle whatever skeletons you and Mercy have, to keep you company."

He rolled his eyes. "It's not what you think—I almost guarantee it—but you don't want to hang out with a guy like me."

"Because…?"

"I'm a bad influence." That was as close to the truth as he cared to get. He didn't mind weaving a tale, but he wasn't fond of the one where he almost lost Mercy's friendship.

"'Kay. 'Cause I've never heard that before. I wanted to talk for a few minutes. It wasn't like I was proposing we set up our gift registry." A gust sliced through the night, and she shivered and rubbed her arms.

He shrugged out of his jacket and draped it over her shoulders. And now she was a petite miss in an oversized coat, and that was more tempting. Damn it. He needed to remind himself why this fascination was unhealthy, prove to her she should be disgusted by him, and abide by Mercy's request. "You're not offering the kind of company I prefer."

"And yet, you haven't left."

Good point. Why didn't he let her walk away?

Better question—why were they having this conversation outside? "You've got me curious as to what this is about."

"You said you've helped people deal with performance issues." She cringed and bit her bottom lip. "You know what I mean."

Because sometimes he didn't know when to shut his mouth and walk away. This time he'd do it consciously, though. He'd deter her once and for all. "I do know. And I was talking specifically about fucking on camera."

She didn't flinch. "You also said there was more to it. How does it work?"

"You don't want details, Suzie-Q. It's all about debauchery and fetish and getting off in public." This way he could convince himself he'd warned her. It was hard to tell if the pink on her cheeks was embarrassment or from the cold. Either way, she'd ask for more information, then realize her mistake, and the discussion would be over.

"And there's got to be a universal principal in there somewhere. *Something* I can use. I'll filter out the screwing and process the rest," she said.

"All right." He moved closer, blocking out her intoxicating scent and ignoring the heat flowing between them.

To her credit, she held his gaze and didn't back away.

"Because each person needs a customized motivation, I'll give you an example." He knew the perfect explicit memory. "When I first got started doing this, and I was only a blog with an *Adult Warning* banner and a login page, I met a girl in Brazil. Gorgeous body. Dark skin. And the things she did with her tongue…"

Susan didn't flinch.

He pushed forward. "She was flexible as fuck. Knew exactly how to hold herself for the perfect shot, and—*Jesus*—her pussy was gorgeous. She insisted she wanted to do porn, but she froze every time I grabbed the camera. She loved to dance. Wasn't as graceful or talented as you. Nowhere near the same league. But she could move to a good club mix like nobody's business. We went out one night, and I made one request when we got there."

"Okay?" Susan flicked her tongue over her bottom lip, watching him.

"She had to take off her panties. She hesitated, but the beat called and the room was dark. No one would know but her and me. The dancing was awkward at first. She couldn't lose herself in the music. *Fuck*, it made me hard, though. When she found her rhythm, the bumping and grinding was more intense than it had ever been. It was as though having that secret between us cut a ribbon of restraint inside her. The way she pressed into me… I wanted to fuck her on the dance floor. I didn't care who saw."

The story was an old one. A tale Andrew used to shock and impress at industry gatherings. He'd told it so many times, it didn't do anything for him anymore. Except tonight, it had his dick harder than one of the icicles hanging from the roof, and he wasn't to the happy ending yet. Some of his arousal had to do with his audience. Susan wasn't shivering under his jacket anymore. The sides had fallen open, and the satin of her dress pressed into her breasts with each breath. Her lips were parted ever so slightly, and those clear blue eyes threatened to capture him.

There was more to the story, and she'd lose interest in him once things got too nasty. That was the point. "She spun and dug her ass into me, and I inched up her skirt to slide my hand between her legs. I expected her to pull away, but she pressed harder. She was so fucking wet. I pushed two fingers inside her, and she rode my hand while the entire club carried on around us. I led her to a booth near the back of the room. The place was crowded, so it wasn't exactly isolated, but it was dark. She was lost in the moment. Didn't care.

"She slid my zipper down and worked my cock free, and when she wrapped her lips around it, I almost came. She was kneeling close to me, so I could tease her clit, and I played with her until she was groaning against my shaft. Squirming. Sucking me off. Climaxing and not caring that a couple of guys at the bar watched the entire thing. When I squirted in her mouth, she licked me clean. Kissed me hard and hungry. Sucked her juices from my fingers. As the euphoria faded, she realized we had an audience and they were entranced. She shoved my hand back between her legs and begged me to make her come again. Never had problems in front of the camera after that." It was only a tale. Words he'd memorized from telling it so often. Simplified, to make a point. So why couldn't he get his hard-on to stop begging for attention?

Far, far worse was that Susan never looked away. Her pupils were dilated, and her lips flushed red. *God damn it.* She was turned on. "Do most of the stories go that way?" she asked.

"That's a tame one." He tried to focus on the cold. To wrap himself in discomfort and chase away the fire searing through his veins. It wasn't the story that had him hornier than he'd been in ages; it was her reaction. "Disgusting, isn't it?"

"I… um… Wow. What if you got caught? There were really people watching?"

This was doing exactly the opposite of what he hoped, and he couldn't find the desire to change it. "Is that really such a big deal? They were enjoying themselves. Participating at a distance. Stroking—" He bit off the words before he could make things worse. He forced his hands into his pockets, rather than give into the impulse to drag a thumb over her bottom lip.

Summoning the last of his willpower, he reached past lust and desire and the urge to press her against a nearby wall and find out what she was or wasn't wearing under her dress. He grabbed the point of the conversation instead. "Anyway, that's how it works. Some people already know how to perform in public, but anyone can learn."

"And that's how you teach your actors to get over the camera fright?"

"Public blowjobs? Sometimes." He ground his teeth, to keep any more unfiltered words from coming out. She obviously didn't have a problem with the conversation, but he promised Mercy…

"There's more to it than that." Susan was like a dog with a bone.

He winced mentally at the poor choice of words. "There's a lot more to it."

"Teach me."

"No."

"Just like that?" Her lower lip stuck out in a pout.

Which shouldn't be enticing, but fuck if he didn't want to nip at her mouth. "Preemptively and completely. No."

"It's because of Mercy, isn't it?"

"It is." Andrew wondered if this was as much about keeping his distance from Susan at this point

—removing the temptation—but it sounded as good as any answer.

"Because after all these years, you love her and would do anything for her?"

The oversimplification of the situation helped him grasp more sensibility. "Sure. If it makes you stop asking, why the fuck not?"

"You're right." She shrugged out of his coat and handed it over. "I don't want to put you at odds with my sister." She passed him. "Now that I know what I'm asking for, I'll find someone else to help me."

Manipulative, clever, seductive— "Like whom?" Simply because his solution to what *she was asking for* sounded like it revolved around public sex, he wouldn't be the first one to flinch.

"You're not the only person who understands stage fright in its various incarnations. I'm sure someone out there would be happy to help a girl like me get over it."

"You're baiting me."

She turned to face him again. "Who? Me?" The tiny smirk that danced on her face both infuriated and enticed him.

"It's not going to work."

"And if I ask the wrong person, and that someone takes advantage of my naïveté, it's on me."

"Technically, it's on them, though I suspect you'd suffer more. I'm calling your bluff. Go find someone else. Have fun with that."

"I'm not bluffing." The pout and wide eyes and bid for pity vanished from her expression. "Have you ever wanted anything so badly, you could taste it in everything? Every breath. Every touch. Every sound. So much that it haunted you and refused to leave you alone?"

Reason kicked on in time to point out he shouldn't go with the facetious answer. He swallowed his, *You. Right now.* "You won't like how the process works."

"I've practiced several hours a day for more than fifteen years. Forgoing sleep. Giving up a social life. Stumbling into the studio at four in the morning, to fit it into my schedule, and spending the rest of the day sore for it. I don't have to like the details, as long as it gets the results I want."

"And doesn't compromise your morals?"

She drew her lips into a thin line. "I don't think you have a good grasp on what those are." Gone was the timid girl, and the determined woman in front of him was no less alluring.

If she saw this as a business transaction, it wouldn't be anything else. That would make it easier.

"You have to follow my instructions to the letter," he said.

"If I don't?"

"Then the process doesn't work, and there's no reason to continue. You either want this, or you don't. I'm already going to say *yes*. Don't make me change my mind before we begin."

"All right. I'm in." Her smile returned, confident and unwavering. "When do we start?"

He shook his head. "One more thing. You don't tell Mercy."

"Because I want this to end before it starts? She's leaving on her honeymoon tonight. She won't hear it from me."

"Perfect. Tomorrow, one in the afternoon, meet me at the R&T offices. Wear comfortable clothes." The offices would be closed since it was Sunday.

He was so fucked if this went south, but with the pleased determination on her face, he couldn't tell her *no*.

SEVEN

SUSAN SAT IN HER CAR IN THE EMPTY R&T PARKING lot, struggling to keep her thoughts from rambling out of control. Not that she'd been successful at any point, since talking to Andrew last night.

She was fifteen minutes early, which meant staring at nothing and letting the chill rake over her. She couldn't stay home alone with her thoughts any longer, though. She hoped getting outside and letting the winter day wrap around her would give her a new place for her focus. She was wrong.

Andrew's story turned her on more than anything ever had. When she got home after the wedding, her panties were soaked. It wasn't that she was completely inexperienced when it came to sex. She'd fooled around with boyfriends and gone as far as third base with a couple of them. She didn't have a problem with the idea of *doing it*; it simply hadn't happened to her yet.

Heck, her vibrator was one of her best friends. She and it caught up real well last night. She lay in bed, Andrew's tale replaying with her mental visuals, while she slid the toy between her legs, stroking, not easing up until she got off twice.

Fantasy continued to tease her today. She'd never understood why people thought public sex—the possibility of getting caught—was a turn on. Now she not only got it, but also wanted to know more.

A sharp rap on her window startled her and pulled her back to the now. She looked up to see Andrew bent at the waist, watching her with a half-formed smile. He gestured for her to join him, so she grabbed her stuff and hopped out of her car.

"I hope I'm not interrupting," he said. "You looked like you were enjoying wherever you were."

A place she was half-tempted and half-terrified to tell him about. "It showed?"

"Don't worry. I'm sure no one else noticed."

Because no one else was around.

He settled a hand on the small of her back and pointed her toward the Range Rover sitting next to her car. The expensive rental was a not-so-subtle reminder that, despite the fact that he wore faded jeans and a hoodie, the man was worth billions. "You ready to become a starlet?"

His question summoned one of her own she'd been trying to ignore since last night. The only hint she had about what his *training* involved was his story. As much as the daydream turned her on, she couldn't be an active participant in that kind of thing. Should she have asked for details? She hadn't wanted to at the time. She was too busy being smug that she convinced him to help her. No reason to jinx it.

"Suzie-Q?" He waved a hand in front of her face. "You ready?"

"Yes." She cringed at the squeak that struggled out. She cleared her throat. "Absolutely." This time she managed more confidence.

He held the door open for her, and waited until she was in the SUV before extending his hand. "Phone. Turn it off first."

"Excuse me?" She might be a bit uncertain about this. Feeling a bit timid. But it wasn't as though she was attached to her Android. Though maybe a little.

"We do this without distractions. My rules—remember?"

Like she could forget. If he were anyone else, she wouldn't agree, and not only because she hated the thought of surrendering the artificial appendage. She typed out a quick text before shutting off the device and handing it over. "That went to my B.F.F., Olivia. If she doesn't hear from me by tonight, she's calling the cops."

"You don't trust me." He didn't look offended as he pocketed her phone.

"It if it weren't for how well Mercy knows you, I'd tell you *no*. So I trust you *enough*."

"But you want to do this anyway."

"That doesn't mean I have to be stupid about it."

He smirked. "I like the way you think. Shall we?"

"Let's." She swallowed, hoping to quell the churning in her gut, and settled back into her seat, while he made his way to the driver's side.

Silence fell between them, as they drove to the main road and then onto the freeway. Were they not allowed to be friendly? Andrew didn't strike her as a nothing-to-say kind of guy. Was it only her he didn't want to talk to? Screw that. Unless it was one of his *rules*, she wasn't spending this entire affair in awkward silence. "How did you get started in your work?" Jobs were a reasonable topic, *and* she got to prove she wasn't a fragile, innocent flower that needed to be sheltered.

"The fucking part or the selling-it part?" He glanced at her out of the corner of his eye, then turned his attention back to the road.

"There's more to it than doing sex stuff and posting it online."

He raised his brow. "Not really. I took the pictures, the participants signed the release, and I happened to have a best friend who was brilliant at getting my content in front of people willing to pay for it."

"And that's it?" Susan didn't expect the casual dismissal of his work. If she asked Dad or any of his friends or their sons about their jobs, she was guaranteed an immeasurable diatribe about their invaluable contributions to the business world. She preferred Andrew's way.

"Do you want me to go on about ROI and contracts and copyright law? Or are you looking for another tale like last night's?"

Was she? Not consciously, though she did like the idea. No. That would be too distracting. She shrugged. "I figure it's an empire; it couldn't have been easy to build."

"It wasn't, but it helps that I love my work. Yes, I mean *the sex stuff.*"

"Don't make fun." The childish retort slipped out before she could stop it.

"Wouldn't dream of it. But I promise it's like any other job. We work long hours when we have to, and the stories about out-of-control orgies are mostly to impress investors."

She couldn't stop her laugh. "Mostly?"

"It's business, Suzie-Q. Someone's always

looking to fuck as many people as they can at once without getting in trouble."

So cynical. She shook her head in amusement. "I don't have a counter for that."

"People rarely do. Tell me—what kind of work are you in, that has you sneaking in rehearsal during lunch and at early hours?"

"I intern at my dad's commercial real-estate firm. It's only temporary, until I graduate and land some dance work."

"I didn't realize you were in school. You don't strike me as a business-major kind of person, but I don't know you that well."

"I'm majoring in fine arts. Online classes. He's got me fetching coffee, running errands—stuff like that." It was decent work. Kept her busy. Kept him happy.

A frown ghosted across Andrew's face. "But *intern* implies he doesn't pay you."

"Well, no. I get free room and board." She chuckled, the same way she always did when explaining work, but this time it didn't feel right. A whisper of anger snaked through her. Who was Andrew, to cast judgment on her? She swallowed the errant thought. He hadn't, and she was overreacting. "It's kind of weak, not having my own money, but the job market is slim for someone without qualifications, and it's only temporary." Now she was over-explaining herself. She stopped short of revealing Dad's teasing threats to kick her out if she got a dancing job.

Andrew's phone rang, and relief tickled her senses at the reprieve. "I had to turn mine off..." she said in a playful tone.

He glanced at the screen for half a second. "And I should have done the same, but I have to get this. It goes off after. I promise." Into the receiver, he said, "Hey, sis."

Then— "I don't really have an opening in my schedule today." Irritation leaked into his words, and Susan turned her attention to the side window, trying not to eavesdrop but not having much of a choice. "I know it's a weekend, but I have plans. I'm half here on vacation... Of course I want to see both of you." He sighed, and Susan looked back in time to see him glance at her. He gave her a weak smile. "I'm either going to bring a friend, or won't be there for a couple of hours. She's a business associate... Why do you care what she does for a living?"

The conversation continued for a few more minutes, with pleasantries that left a strain in Andrew's voice. By the time he hung up, Susan was all but squirming with curiosity and embarrassment. Was *sis* a nickname, like he seemed to use with everyone, or was it his actual sister? Did whoever it was think Susan was in porn? And why didn't the assumption bother Susan? "Do we need to reschedule?" she asked.

"I'd rather not." He pocketed his phone, then rubbed his face. "I want to see my sister and nephew while I'm here, but their schedule isn't matching mine. If it were anyone else, I'd tell them to fuck off. I promised you my time today. I can either take you back home, or you can go with me. Which would be one of those incredibly awkward, serves-my-sister-right-for-last-minute-planning things, and could be a blast if you're into that kind of stuff. And we can pick this up after."

He cared about his family—he was doing one better than Mercy.

That wasn't fair of Susan. Her sister might have walked away from the people who loved her, out of some misdirected sense of spite, but she was back in their lives now. "I'll go, if you're sure your sister doesn't mind."

ANDREW WAS SURPRISED the tension bled from his neck when Susan didn't ask to go home. "Kandace will love you." *Probably.* "Though she's convinced you're a porn star, and she's going to be floored the first time you say *oh my heck*. She doesn't believe I know respectable people."

"I promise to be on my best behavior."

"I don't doubt it for a second." He was struggling to wrap his head around Susan's thought process. She had the innocence thing going on, and her hesitation made it clear some topics caught her off guard, but she didn't seem to mind them. But there was a break-point, rather than a smooth transition, where bashful became bold. It confounded and fascinated him.

He wanted to go back to their conversation, but she started to close off when he asked about her getting paid for work deterred him. Most of what he knew about their father came from Mercy's perspective, and Andrew had little more than contempt for the man. It wasn't his place to shove that onto Susan if she felt differently. She asked for his help with public performances, not yanking off the rose-colored glasses she saw the world through. "Why dancing?" That should be a good topic.

From the way she sat up straighter and the glow on her face he caught out of the corner of his eye, that was the right question. "I love losing myself in the rhythm. Molding my body to the emotions of the composer and orchestra. Gliding with their passions draws me in. It's hard to describe."

"I disagree. You did a fantastic job. It's a difficult industry to break into, you know. Jobs are seasonal. Pay is sporadic, and frequently not of the living-wage level."

"Jeez. You sound like my dad."

"I hope not." He winced at the words. The last thing he wanted was to be compared to a man who cared more about his family's image in the church pews than their needs and potential.

"You're not changing my mind."

"That's the last thing I want. If you do or don't do it, it should be because of you, not because someone else said so. You should have the facts, though. If you're okay with all of it, then pursue the fuck out of your passion."

"You think so?" Her smile, bright and genuine and sincere, stole his breath and thoughts.

He jammed his brain back into gear. "I agreed to help you, didn't I?"

"Speaking of… How does this work?"

He hadn't figured that out yet. He had a vague idea but was working on the details around how to get her to shed a deeply rooted stage fright without resorting to things like exhibitionism. Having a late lunch with Kandace would buy him some more time. "That's a surprise," he said.

For both of them.

EIGHT

Lucas stared at Susan, eyes wide. Andrew wasn't sure what to make of it, until the boy said, "I love your hair."

"Thanks." She grinned. "My dad hates it, but everyone else likes it. I'm thinking orange next."

"I wish I was that bold." Awe filled Lucas's voice.

"I'm not bold at all."

Lucas leaned closer to her and lowered his voice. "You'll need to learn if you're spending time with him." He nodded at Andrew.

Andrew wasn't sure he wanted to know what that meant. He touched Susan's arm, to draw her attention, and his mind stalled when she turned in his direction. He shook blank thoughts aside. "I need to talk to Kandace for a minute. You two be all right until we get back?"

"Sure." She looked more at home settling onto the leather sofa than he'd ever felt, and he bought the house.

He blocked out her conversation with Lucas, about how she got the blue to stick, and led Kandace into the kitchen.

"She's a little young to be in porn, isn't she?" Kandace asked as soon as they were out of earshot.

He wasn't in the mood for this. "She's twenty-one, she doesn't work for me, and you know not all of my associates fuck for a living."

"I do know it, but to hear you talk, they do. Are you all right?"

"I'm fine. Why?"

"You haven't made a single smart-ass quip since you walked in the door. Are you sick?" She raised the inside of her wrist to his forehead.

He swatted her hand away. "I don't have a fever. And she's Mercy's younger sister."

"Ah."

"What's that supposed to mean?" He winced at the edge in his own words.

Her frown said she noticed. "You really are on edge. What's going on?"

He breathed in, then counted to three as he exhaled, trying to chase away the tension. "I was serious on the phone the other day."

"So was I. No therapy. Whatever we can do to

avoid it." She opened the fridge, grabbed a bottle of water and a beer, and handed him the water.

He accepted but didn't twist off the lid. "We already agreed on that. I mean about telling Lucas the truth. He deserves to know."

"No." At least they weren't dancing around the issue.

"I'm not asking permission. It's going to happen."

She leaned against the counter and took a long drag off her drink, before asking, "Have you thought this through?"

"I've had ten years to think it through. I've never been comfortable with the arrangement." He didn't expect her to yield without a little pushback, but the flat-out refusal caught him off-guard.

"*Never?* You didn't protest too hard."

When he was eighteen, she made good points for telling Lucas she was his mother. Lucas's health and happiness were more important than Andrew's ego. "It's true I've made a lot of excuses, even after I got myself together. But he's reaching an age where he can understand, and he'll be happier if he knows sooner rather than later."

"In your head, how does it play out once you tell him?" She crossed her arms and stared.

There weren't a lot of options he was aware of, when it came to raising a kid. "He goes back to Georgia with me, and I enroll him in a school where they don't tell kids they'll go to hell for wanting to have sex." He didn't want to take Lucas away from home, but if he led with the worst case, they could negotiate from there.

"So you'll take a boy who already thinks his desires are evil, remove him from the only home he's ever known, and plunge him headfirst into the filth that is your world?"

It sounded fucked up when she said it like that. "There's not a lot of filth. The maid comes and cleans the place twice a week. And the pool boy is sexy as hell."

She rolled her eyes and pushed past him. "And now you've deteriorated."

"I'm joking." He grabbed her arm. "Well, I'm not—the house is clean—but where's your sense of humor?"

"You're talking about a human being's future."

"I know." He forced himself to sound serious. "And you're being myopic." He wasn't doing this the way they did ten years ago. He didn't like being pushed out of his son's life then, and he was putting his foot down now. "There's got to be a happy medium on the what-next front."

"You tell me what that is, and we'll talk."

He clenched his jaw and bit back the sarcastic comments that tried to force their way out. "I'm here now, trying to get your input."

"Or what? You'll come back with lawyers and force the issue?"

He stared at her in shock. "Okay... No idea where that came from. You're his family. I get that. You raised him. I don't think this is the kind of secret we can or should keep."

"I'm his mother. I think we should."

"You're his aunt"—Andrew grasped for a reasonable response that didn't imply he was going to yield—"and I'm not going to tell him he should stop calling you *Mom*. But think about it from a bigger-picture angle. How pissed off would you be, if you hit fifteen or twenty or forty and found out your mother lied to you your entire life about who your parents were?"

"But that's not what you're proposing." Desperation leaked into her tone.

"I don't want to break up the family, but we are going to tell him while I'm here, and it's going to have large versions of the truth attached to it." He felt like an ass at the frown she wore. "It doesn't have to be today. I'll do you the same favor you did me back then, and give you a few days to be okay with it. You can approve what I tell him, as long as you don't censor the important details."

Susan's life was littered with awkward dinners. At the country club. For Dad's work. School functions. Church gatherings. But the scowl Andrew wore when he emerged from the kitchen with Kandace unsettled her.

As they sat to eat, the siblings relaxed, and Andrew's joking attitude roared back full force. Lucas spent a lot of time rolling his eyes, but Susan was entertained.

"*Susan*, isn't it?" Kandace turned to her. "I understand you're not in the industry."

"No. I'm a dancer." It felt awkward to claim a job she didn't have yet, but something stopped her from saying, *I intern for my dad.*

Kandace's expression drooped. "I see. I didn't think there were a lot of places for that here."

"It's a tough industry anywhere. But I'm trying to make the season ticket with Ballet West. Once I get my degree, I'm going to teach. I'm hoping junior high or high school."

"Oh." Kandace's eyes grew wide. "You're actually a dancer."

"As opposed to…?"

Andrew gave a snort laugh. "A stripper. Told you she doesn't approve of my associates."

"Could we not do this?" Lucas dropped his face into his hands, muffling the last of his plea.

Susan felt bad for him. Dad embarrassed her all the time, though his comments were more like, *She'll be an old maid soon. I'm hoping someone respectable snatches her up before then.*

"Some of the girls I know from auditions work at Southern Exposure." She could balance a neutral, clean conversation with all sorts of topics. Another thing those awkward dinners taught her. "Some of them do it for money. Most love it. They're totally sweet. But I could never do that; I'd chicken out."

"Me too." Lucas used his fork to chase peas around his plate. He looked up at Susan. "When you do the ballet thing, how do you ignore the eyes on you?"

She didn't. That was the problem. "When I figure that out, I'll let you know."

"Okay." He smiled.

The conversation slid from one topic to the next after that, until Susan and Andrew wished Kandace and Lucas a good evening, and made their way back to Andrew's rental car.

"I like your family," Susan said as they pulled onto the main road. "They remind me of us, when we'd all get together."

"Us?"

"My family." She relaxed in her seat and watched the scenery pass by. Though it was barely five, the sun was vanishing. He made a choking noise, and she glanced at him. "What?" she asked.

He made an exaggerated show of clearing his throat. "Nothing. I don't know them, so I can't say."

"Well you can't go based on anything Mercy told you. She left us behind."

"Right. That's how it went down." He pointed the car toward downtown Salt Lake. "I was going to take you to dinner, but I think we've got that covered. You up for a stroll around The Gateway?"

She wanted to go back to the conversation about what Mercy had said about their family, but she didn't want to spoil the mood. "I'm in." The Gateway was an outdoor mall. All the shops besides the theater and the restaurants would be closed, and it would be chilly, but it was a pretty view regardless. This time of year, it was even better. Besides, she was supposed to do what she was told, and was curious to see what kind of *training* he had in mind.

Silence settled between them, and she frowned. She saw him at the wedding. At the reception desk in R&T. With his sister. He didn't have any problem sliding through quips. She had to get him to drop his guard, to get the same. Did she have Mercy to thank, for him withdrawing? The sarcastic thought burrowed deep, and Susan couldn't ignore it. Didn't matter. Small talk was a must in her world.

"Are you a fan of classic movies?" she asked.

"As in, *Star Wars*? *Pretty in Pink*? Define classic."

"You quoted *Casablanca* then night we met."

"You remember that?" He sounded surprised.

"Should I not?" Far more memories had come back than she cared for. The feeling of helplessness when she realized she lost control of the situation. Her gratitude that he was there to step in. Thinking that she shouldn't like the idea of needing to be saved, but enjoying the rescue anyway.

He paid the parking lot attendant and navigated them toward an empty spot. "Doesn't usually happen with GHB or any of those drugs."

They climbed from the car and made their way toward the shops.

"How do you know so much about it?" she asked.

"Personal experience." Quickly, he added, "Taking, not giving. It's a shame I don't do my own camera work anymore. I'd put you in one of my movies."

The sudden change in subject jarred her, but she switched gears. "I don't remember asking." She wanted to leave it at that, but fantasy surged into her thoughts. Baring it all for an audience. Stripping down, a piece of clothing at a time. Getting off to someone getting off on her. She shoved the images aside. If she kept hanging out with him, she wasn't going to need a coat, regardless of how cold it got outside.

"You didn't. But for as many people as seem to expect that's how we know each other, the idea's got potential."

It had far more than she cared to admit. "I'd be terrified. I don't have a public presence with my clothes *on*. That's why we're here. Remember?"

"Once I'm done with you, that all vanishes. You'll blossom into a star." Confidence leaked from his assurance.

"Really?" She couldn't keep the disbelief from her voice. "You'll not only cure me of my *lacking presence*, but also have me begging to take my clothes off for an audience?"

"*Begging* is exactly the word I would have used, but how'd you know?"

She rolled her eyes, but she was laughing. "I notice you didn't answer my question."

His step faltered for half a second. His smug expression never slipped. "What question?"

"Are you a fan of classic movies?"

"*Behind the Green Door, The Devil in Miss Jones...* Sure. Love all that stuff."

She dragged the titles through her memory, to find any connection at all. "Is that the one where the billionaire poses as a clerk in his own shoe store? Romantic comedy 1940's style?"

"*In* Miss Jones, not *and* Miss Jones. Classic tale about a woman who spends her entire life obeying the rules, and then kills herself in a fit of frustration."

"That sounds horrible."

"Not done yet." He held up a finger. "Despite all

her good deeds, that one final act damns her to hell, where she's subjected to all manner of debauchery and pleasure. Or—if you'd prefer—a movie about sex stuff."

She was never going to live that down, but she wasn't going to give him another opportunity to poke fun at her innocence. "Don't know if I'd prefer it or not, though I'd rather not wait until I was dead to find out."

"Probably smart. By the end of the movie, she's addicted to the pleasure, and her eternal punishment after that is to never get off again. If you play your cards right, you get the bad-sex and not-getting-off parts out of the way early in adulthood, and figure out how to enjoy everything that comes after. Which includes you, over and over, if you're doing it right."

Her face heated to red-hot. Keeping him from uncovering her lack of experience was easier said than done. Especially if he was the one doing the saying.

NINE

Andrew learned early in life that humor was one of the best ways to mask an awkward situation. Pulling up the jokes and distracting conversation when Susan hit too close to uncomfortable with questions about his past was instinct, but he recognized what he was doing as soon as the first words were out of his mouth. He was pretty sure *little sister* wasn't as innocent as Mercy believed, but those moments when the pink dots formed on Susan's cheeks short-circuited his off switch.

He slowed his step to watch her walk. It was a fantastic view. Her jeans hugged her ass, and she had a casual grace he'd rarely seen. The holiday lights sparkling like a million multi-colored stars surrounded her in an angelic-like glow.

. . .

"Serious question." Her voice tugged him back to the conversation, and she paused to let him catch up.

"I can't promise a serious answer with a lead-in like that, but I'll try."

"Why porn?" There was a brief hesitation when she said *porn*. It could have been a stutter or a catch in her throat.

He didn't think either was the case. "Asking the question a different way than last time doesn't mean you get a different answer."

They reached the center of the plaza, where a high wall curved up to meet the second floor and created an amphitheater out of the bricks below. In the summer, it was an open fountain, with jets of water dancing toward the sky at random intervals. Now it was a crystal half-cave, glinting in Christmas lights and reflecting the full moon, and circled with benches. When she whirled to face him, her body flowed. She managed to turn the simplest step into a pirouette.

"I'm not the only one who's asked," she said. "You've got a stock reply. Easy answer is, *I'm a guy; I like naked stuff.*"

He frowned. He did have a party-version of the story on hand, specifically for questions like *why porn*.

"But I'm thinking you're about twenty-eight, like Mercy," Susan said.

"Yes. We're the same age."

"So you were my age when you kicked the whole thing off."

"Which makes me sound ancient. It was only seven years ago." *Jesus.* He felt like a dirty old man, lusting after someone so young. He'd hoped to hold out until forty or longer before that happened. That had to be it. He projected some sort of misplaced opportunity from his early twenties on her. Another reason to add to his *Why Susan is Off Limits* list, right under *for Mercy.*

She stuck out her tongue. "I can do the math. Thanks. My point is I haven't finished school. I can't get the job I want. My future is a huge blur. You'd already spent three years exploring the world, and you decided to build a billion-dollar empire because you like masturbation?"

"Yup. That's how it happened. I woke up one day and said, *I like naked people. So does everyone else. I'm going to be a billionaire.*" He kept the teasing in his sarcasm.

"Exactly. You didn't do anything like that. So, once again, why porn?"

"It was a bit like that, but I didn't expect to make any money from it. Why do you want to know?"

She furrowed her brow and tilted her head to the side, studying him. "Because it's about you." She made it sound as if the answer was obvious.

He had no idea what to do with the statement. "It's not this great and grandiose tale of victory and smart business." No. This wasn't how the script went. "When I first got to Argentina, I lied my way into a bed or fifty, saying I was a talent scout from the U.S. It was how I found places to sleep." No, no, *no*. His version of how it happened was far flashier.

"Did women actually buy that?" She didn't look disgusted or bothered. The same open curiosity she had the night of the wedding shone on her face.

"I'm pretty sure they didn't," came out instead of *Always. I was a smooth mother fucker.* Damn it. He didn't know where he was in the script anymore. The problem was, he'd delivered it so many times, he wasn't even certain what the truth was.

He could get close, though. "It was sleazy. It was effective as fuck. It didn't matter they didn't buy it, they liked the way I pulled the line off without flinching. I had a whole spiel, including a photocopied release form, *in case* they made my list. One day, someone called me on it. I'd drunk too much tequila, promised her all sorts of fame and fortune, and she wanted to see the site she was on. I wanted back in her bed in the near future, so I tossed a few pages together, convinced Mercy to hide them behind a login, and threw some of my other pictures up there, to make it look authentic."

"Let me guess. This doesn't end with you

learning your lesson on account of her knowing the site was fake."

"Not even close. We played out the ruse too well. Mercy did a bang-up job with the search-engine optimization. Landed the right keywords without meaning to. My photos were incredible, and suddenly our shitty payment portal and handful of images were bringing in money. Not much. It kept us in bus tickets, and hotel rooms instead of hostels. But God damn, if I didn't get more tail than I thought possible, when I actually *was* the guy who owned *that one adult site*."

Susan fiddled with the button on the cuff of her jacket, her gaze focused on the bricks.

An unfamiliar sensation tugged inside Andrew. Was he embarrassing her? Why did he care? "Anyway. From there, we spun it into a venture where I could pay other people. Mercy worked her magic, getting the various sites out there. I designed the layouts and set the fetish guidelines. The rest fell like pretty much any other business plan."

"But you love what you do." She looked up, and her gaze bored into him, as if she could read below the surface.

"Naked people and fucking. We covered that."

"It's more than that. You enjoy what it represents. Being open. Letting people express themselves."

He shook his head. "You've got a lot more faith

in my intentions than they deserve. By the way…
we're not here for me. Don't think I missed that
you've turned the attention away from you."

"NOT ON PURPOSE." Susan swallowed her
frustration. Everything with Andrew was counter,
block, and parry. Each time she caught a glimpse of
what lay underneath, he covered it up with a new
flash and distraction. Worse, she didn't understand
why she kept poking, prodding, and digging. She'd
coerced him into doing her this favor, playing off
some twisted attachment he had to her sister. What
more did she need to know, as long as they both
accomplished their goals?

"Now that we're back on topic, I'd like to see
you dance," he said.

"You've seen me dance." The notion twisted her
gut in knots. What if he thought less of her, once he
had a chance to see her for more than a few
seconds? What if she screwed up? What if Dad was
right, and this was a waste of time? Familiar doubts
pressed in and threatened to suffocate her, but she
clawed her way past them. She'd asked for his help
with this; she wasn't going to tell him *no*. "But if you
meet me back at R&T early tomorrow, I'm happy to
do an on-demand performance."

"You misunderstand. I want to see it now."

"Here?" Her question came out as a squeak. People passed by in groups of two or five or more, on their way to dinner or the movies. This time of year, with so many holiday shoppers lingering despite the closed stores, it was far from being a private show.

Andrew moved close enough that heat flowed between them, but he never made contact. "I dated a guy once. Super uptight. Formal. Complete control freak." His voice rolled over her with a current of electricity. "But—Jesus—he could fuck."

"Like on camera?" Stupid question. That was what most of his stories were about.

"Like on me. He wasn't an actor. The man knew how to get me off."

Andrew never flinched, and neither would she. The problem was she was now fantasizing about him with another man, and that was distracting. Picturing Andrew stripped down, some well-built guy kissing him, stroking him— "Is this another story that ends with you getting a blow job on a bench?" She was grateful she kept her question steady and neutral.

"No. Do you want to hear it or not?"

"Yes."

"I took him out to dinner one night. I was enjoying the new feeling of having a free cash flow. It was a super classy place—or I thought so at the time. French version of Olive Garden, but with American food."

She'd been to France and was pretty sure such a thing didn't exist, but she didn't dare interrupt and stop the tale.

"Or—you know—it was a little café on the corner somewhere, but they had tablecloths and candlelight, so it felt classy. We placed our orders, and chatted while we waited. He had a little wine. Wasn't sitting quite as straight as normal. I dropped my hand to his leg and glided it up to his zipper. He pushed me away, but the right coaxing convinced him no one could see."

She tried to swallow, but her throat was dry. "And?"

He flicked his gaze across her face and gave a tiny shake of his head. "When I worked his cock free from his jeans, it was so hard I could cut glass with it and his spine went just as rigid. But the company was good, and his dick was hot against my palm, so I took my time stroking him."

Details splashed with images through her thoughts, making her pulse race. Desire thrummed under her skin and throbbed between her legs. This was better than Tumblr.

"As the anticipation built, he relaxed." If Andrew had any idea the effect he was having on her, it didn't show. "When he tilted his head back, eyes half closed, I knew he was lost in the moment. He groaned when he came. Made a mess of my hand. Drew stares and more than a few whispers from the people around us. I guarantee, not all of them were as disgusted as they were acting."

She didn't know if she was more embarrassed for the unnamed boyfriend, or jealous. Temptation urged her to excuse herself for a few minutes, find the nearest bathroom, and slip her fingers between her legs. "What happened next?"

"Management asked us to leave, because we were disrupting the other diners."

"Oh my heck, why would you tell me that?" There was no way she was dancing here now.

He raised an eyebrow. "It made you hot and bothered, and I like the memory."

"I thought you were trying to convince me to do a command performance."

"I am." He leaned his head in, and his hot breath sent tantalizing shivers down her spine. "What's holding you back?"

"What if it pisses someone off?"

He looked her in the eye, but his nearness jumbled her thoughts. "That's a worst-case scenario. The story is important because, aside from being sent to jail or getting beaten up for being queer— neither of which is an option here—there wasn't a lot more that could happen. It didn't kill us, and it left us both with a fantastic memory."

"But it's so embarrassing." The argument sounded weak, and she was the one saying it.

He slid behind her and rested his hands on her hips. When he pressed against her back, his hard length told her she wasn't the only one turned on. "You want to be a performer." He dragged his nose along the back of her neck as he spoke. "Perform."

She swallowed a whimper. "There's no music." She hovered on the knife's edge, between paralyzing fear and intense desire. If he teased his fingers under the waistband of her jeans, she'd have a difficult time saying *no*. But she couldn't imagine dancing here, with so many people around.

He removed one of his hands from its resting spot, and seconds later, a heavy dance beat spilled from behind her. She assumed it came from his phone. People turned to look, muttering to each other.

Humiliation flooded her. "Please stop."

"I told you how this works." His lips moved against her skin. "You do things by my rules, or we call it quits. If you stop now, we're done. I'll take you home, and we won't speak of this again." He swayed her hips to the beat, moving with her.

It felt forced. She couldn't bring herself to do anything more than respond mechanically. Too many thoughts pressed in on her at once, fuzzing the world around her, until all she saw were the stares and all she felt was him.

"Stop caring what they think. What you want is all that matters." His voice was low and hypnotic.

"It doesn't work that way."

"Focus on my voice and the music. Ignore the people. Block out the rest of the world."

Temptation mingled with desire and embarrassment, racing through her. Clouding her mind. Humming in her head and over her body.

"I can't." She pulled out of his grasp but couldn't turn to look at him.

The music vanished. He didn't respond. Her heart hammered in her ears, as seconds ticked away. Why wasn't he saying anything? She whirled to see him walking toward the parking lot.

She sprinted to catch up and tugged the sleeve of his jacket. "I'm sorry."

"If you're not serious, you're wasting your time and mine."

"I am serious. I told you I want this. I'll do it. Stop, please."

"No."

"Why not?" Her throat was raw with frustration.

He didn't look at her. "I can prompt you. Coerce you. Encourage you and go so far as to seduce you. But at the end of the day, if you do this for anyone's approval except your own, you're doing it for the wrong reasons."

"I want to try. Please? I'm doing it for me. I

promise." She pulled him to a stop. "*Damn it.* Look at me."

He spun and grabbed her wrist, locking his gaze on hers. "If you lie about this, to me or yourself, it doesn't work." The smooth tone was gone from his voice.

The power in his grip terrified and excited her. She refused to look away. "I'm not lying." She was, though. The idea of doing this still terrified her. Did it show?

Expression going flat, he let go and turned away. "I don't know how many ways I can say this. You didn't follow my rules. We're done. We have to work in the morning, it's more than a half-hour drive up the canyon, and you have to tell your B.F.F. nothing horrible happened to you. We should go."

TEN

ANDREW DIDN'T FALL ASLEEP UNTIL THE EARLY hours of Monday morning. Nothing, including beating off, appealed to him. The moment with Susan replayed in his head, until exhaustion relegated the thoughts to dream status.

Now he sat in his temporary office at R&T, doing everything he could to think about work, and failing completely. He managed to avoid Susan this morning. It was a small thing, but one to be grateful for.

He pushed too hard last night. Prodded more than was reasonable, given her insecurities. He didn't know why. Regardless of his reasons, the arrangement was over now. Odds were she wouldn't make good on her bluff to find other help. She would have already done that if it were an option— and why was he dwelling on this?

He shoved the thoughts aside and turned back to the hardware contracts his IT team wanted him to review. He wouldn't meet with Mercy's people until this afternoon, so he had time to find his creative center.

Forty-five minutes later, when his phone rang, he'd read the same paragraph about warranty and repair scheduling five times, and he still had no idea what it said. "Yeah?" He answered, attention focused on the contract.

"Happy Monday." Kandace sounded far too chipper for his liking.

"I've had better. I've had worse. Calling me three times in a week? This is a record for you. You miss me that much?"

Her chuckle sounded as forced as his attempt at levity. "Trust me. I wish I wasn't calling," she said.

"Is Lucas all right?" His mind was completely—mostly—off Susan.

"For now. I'm fine too, thanks for asking."

"What does *for now* mean?"

She sighed. "On his way out the door this morning, he announced he's doing the therapy. I pointed out all the things I discussed with him—the reasons it was harmful. He told me that wouldn't be a problem for him, because he's broken and this will fix him."

"*Jesus.*" Andrew didn't know what else to say. He'd seen the after effects of the therapy in actors.

In friends. The process started with stripping away a patient's sense of self. The side-effect was intense self-loathing. From there, the therapist *rebuilt* the patient into someone who wasn't attracted to the same sex. Or really, anything at all.

Andrew lost an actress to suicide because of the resulting self-hatred, several years back. "We can't let him."

"I hate to phrase it this way, but it's his choice."

"So you agree with him?" Andrew swallowed the bile rising in his throat.

"*No*. But forbidding him from going isn't going to make the situation better. I figured he'd attend a session or two, and the urge to rebel—or whatever this is—would pass."

Shittiest plan ever. "He won't go to any sessions at all."

"You don't get to backseat parent."

"Great. That solves two issues. I'm stepping in, we're putting a stop to this, and the conversation is over."

"All right." She sounded tired.

Andrew pulled the phone from his ear and stared at it in disbelief for a second, before holding it back to his head. "Say that again. I think we've got a bad connection."

"You can tell him you're his father. I won't fight you on it. But I'm not agreeing to anything else until we know how that goes."

"What are you up to?" It wasn't that his sister was manipulative, but in ten years, she'd never budged on the issue. This was too easy.

"I'm serious when I say I don't want Lucas doing this." Frustration joined her exhaustion. "I don't know what else to try, so if this makes a difference, it's worth it. Besides, he needs to know sooner rather than later. You're right about that."

"Say that again."

"Knock it off." She gave a tiny laugh. "Can you come down Saturday morning?"

"I'll be there." As he hung up, his mind whirred at the development. Sure, this was one of his goals, but he never expected her to up and say *all right.* He was prepared to fight and argue and run into a brick wall regardless.

Now he had no idea what he was supposed to say to Lucas. *Hi, kid. I'm not actually your uncle; I'm your biological father. Surprise. Let's go get ice cream. Strip club will wait until you're legal.* Yeah, he was going to need to work on that. At least he had a few days to get it right. *Please let me get it right.*

SUSAN COULDN'T HOLD back the yawn that threatened to split her jaw. Her eyes watered, and she did her best to wipe them dry without smearing her eyeliner. She'd had to get up an hour earlier than normal, to drive into the valley, so she could practice before work. In a few days, she might summon the courage to risk running into Andrew. Or she'd steer clear of R&T until he was gone.

She yawned again. It sucked she couldn't drink coffee on the clock without drawing a glare and disapproving sniff from Dad. Fortunately, it was lunchtime, she was meeting Olivia, and she was getting all the espresso and all the sweet to mask the bitter.

Susan parked in the lot one street over from Main Street, and made her way to the café where her lunch plans waited. Olivia was outside. They hugged, exchanged basic hello, and were seated. Susan ordered the biggest, strongest iced coffee on the menu, despite the temperature outside.

"Long night?" Olivia asked, a teasing glint in her eye.

"Not the way you're thinking. How was Phoenix?"

"Hot. Dry. But promising. I should know in a couple of days if I got the job or not."

"That's awesome." Susan hated to see another friend leave for distant places, but this was an amazing opportunity, and she hoped it panned out for Olivia.

Olivia poked an ice cube with her straw, and bubbles from her Coke fizzed around it. "What about you? How was the wedding? Fill me in on *everything*. Give me substance to block out a week straight of job interviews and schmoozing."

So many responses ran through Susan's head. The last week held more than she cared to think about. Mercy's wedding, of course. The near-assault at the steakhouse. The failed audition with Ballet West. Instead of any of that, what came out was, "I met a guy."

"But last night wasn't that kind of night? He's a *guy* guy, then? Not a fuck-toy guy?"

"Neither." Now that Susan had a few extra seconds to assemble her thoughts, she could talk intelligently. One of the reasons she loved Olivia was there was no judgement about Susan's sex life or lack thereof. Olivia understood the desire to find someone but not rush into getting laid. "A little bit the latter. But really, neither. He's a friend of Mercy's."

"In town for the wedding? Sounds *a lot* like the second."

"He's a business partner. Her friend from when she traveled."

Olivia's eyes grew wide. "Porn guy?"

"One and the same." She considered asking Olivia not to call him that to his face, but Andrew would probably be amused by it.

"So serious fuck-toy-ability."

Susan nearly said *I wish*, and the sentiment caught her off-guard. Did she? It might be nice, learning from someone with that kind of experience. Who was she kidding? It would probably be amazing, but that didn't make it a good idea. "Except that I'm his best friend and business partner's little sister. But I mean it—not like that." She related the past week of awkward run-ins but left out his stories that kept her company at night. She wasn't sure why. Probably because she didn't want to paint the situation as anything other than what it was, but definitely not because she liked the idea of keeping the tales for herself.

"So, basically, I found this one person who says he knows how to help me get past the mental block keeping me from getting a dancing job, and what did I do? Chickened out like a Class-A coward." Susan hated admitting it.

Olivia raised her brows. "It sounds like he was a first-class ass."

"He was. He is. I think he prefers it that way. But I know what he was going for, and when I think about it, it wouldn't have killed me to do what he said. Not that there's a chance of it ever coming up again. He and I are done." He made that vividly clear.

"If he said *yes* once, he'll do it again. You simply need a buffer."

Susan stared at her, trying to make sense of the suggestion. "A what, now?"

"Someone else there to keep him from pushing

your buttons." Olivia made it sound like the answer was obvious.

That was such a bad idea, it wasn't on the scale of worth considering. "I'm pretty sure the bigger his audience, the better. A buffer means he'll seek out more embarrassing buttons."

"Not for him. For you. People who have your back, so you don't feel isolated."

If Susan had friends around, she wouldn't feel so out of sorts. Not that she thought he'd agree to the suggestion. Andrew seemed pretty set on the concept of his rules—his way. "What did you have in mind?"

"Jodie's party, tomorrow night."

"I don't know…"

"Up to you." Olivia shrugged. "If you think he has the solution to you landing a gig, beg him for another chance. Personally, I think he sounds like a pushy asshole, in that really sexy, dominant kind of way. If you're not interested in him, you can introduce me."

Susan swallowed the surge of jealousy that rose in her throat. "He's all yours, as long as it doesn't hurt what I'm trying to accomplish."

"Is that a *yes*, then?"

"I'll see what he says." It was a generic brush-off. As she said it, Susan knew she wouldn't ask Andrew for another chance. Regardless of how many friends would be there, to watch her back.

She and Olivia chatted through lunch and dessert about everything under the sun—Olivia's job prospects, Susan's goals for applying for a master's program, and whatever else came up.

Susan put the conversation with Olivia out of her head the moment she got back to work. Or tried to. The idea taunted her at the most inconvenient times. When someone was asking her a question. As she was in the middle of answering phones. She forced herself to drive straight home after work, refusing to take a detour to R&T or Andrew's hotel.

She poured her attention into homework and studying that night, and by the time she climbed into bed, the hectic day plus the lack of sleep the night before tugged her eyelids shut.

That didn't mean sleep came. Every time she opened her eyes, it was only minutes since she last checked the clock. She finally drifted off around two, and when her alarm woke her at four, so she could get to the dance studio before work, she was ready to say *screw it*.

She hit *Snooze*, and dragged herself out of bed closer to seven. That meant no time to practice, but perhaps she could catch Andrew. Exhaustion had removed her I-care filter, so it seemed like the perfect time to approach him.

He wasn't there when she arrived at eight. She didn't have to be to work until nine but had no idea what kind of hours he kept or if he was coming in at all. It wouldn't hurt to wait around for five or ten minutes. She let herself into his office and settled into the chair on the other side of the desk. The room looked sparse. Bare walls. Empty folder bins. A laptop and mousepad decorated the desk. He probably intended to be back at some point.

She folded her arms, settled them on the polished wood surface, and rested her cheek on them, gaze attached to the wall.

"Hey, sleepy head." A gentle voice drilled into her thoughts and dragged her from a dream. A warm hand on her shoulder shook her until her head rattled, and she jerked up with a start.

Andrew stepped back, hands in the air, amusement on his face. "Didn't mean to startle you. Is there a reason you're sleeping in my office?"

"I'm not sleeping." She struggled to grasp her language skills, and forced her brain to feed her words that made sense.

He took his seat across from her. "Resting your eyes. I get it. I'm surprised to see you here. I didn't think you were speaking to me."

"You're the one who said we were through."

"Heat of the moment. It's passed." He looked as calm as he sounded. He also wore that darned impassive mask that meant he'd put up an invisible wall between them. "Things will be awkward if we do the not-talking thing. Mercy will ask why. Someone might tell her the truth…"

This wasn't going the way she needed it to. Not that she had the brain power to know how that was. "Give me another chance, please?"

"Nope. Thanks for stopping by. I have work to do. You know your way out, I assume." He flipped up the lid of his laptop.

"Please?"

"It's a worse idea than the first time you asked me."

"I'm begging." *Why?* Because she wanted this— the help he could provide. It had nothing to do with wanting him in her life a little longer in general. "No emotional blackmail or manipulation. I'll get down on my knees if that'll help." She stood.

"*No.*" He spoke through clenched teeth. "That will most certainly not help. Sit down." He'd stopped shooing her out. This was a good sign.

"I know the perfect place. It'll be crowded. Lots of people. Plenty of chance for public"—she stopped herself from saying *humiliation*; that approach wouldn't help her cause—"displays."

"You think you get to pick? Is this some sort of gathering of your friends?"

"I know the girl celebrating. I won't know most of the people there."

"From church?"

She hadn't been to church since she was sixteen. "From school. She got accepted into a master's program at Stanford."

He drummed his fingers on the desk, and she bit the inside of her cheek to keep from tossing in another round of pleading. When he said, "All right," she let out a breath she didn't realize was holding.

"Thank you. Thank you." She wanted to leap across the desk and hug him but restrained herself.

"Save the gratitude until you know if this actually works. Tell me where to meet you and when to be there."

ELEVEN

Andrew stood on the sidewalk, near the buildings and out of the flow of traffic. On his left was the restaurant where Susan said they were meeting. People in their early twenties arrived in groups of two and three. How many friends did this master's student friend of hers have? He didn't know why he agreed to her request. Though, when she offered to get down on her knees, the assault of images jumbled his brain to the point of temporary insanity.

A tiny part of him was willing to admit he didn't like the idea of a rift between them. He couldn't say why though, and that bothered him.

On his other side, people arrived for what seemed to be a company holiday party. Conversations overlapped and blended in a disjointed symphony.

"I heard some of the new people from Aror-Tech's Chicago office will be here. Replacements, possibly"

"I can't wait for winter break, but the last-minute exams are killing me"

"Open bar this year. For once. Only good thing to come out of this buy-out"

"I'm going before the thesis board in February. There's no way I'll be ready"

"I can't believe we're having the company party on a weeknight. Especially with so many of us who live in the valley"

"Did you hear why Jodie picked Stanford over BYU?"

"Everyone's saying admin screwed up booking, but I hear they're doing it on a Tuesday because Chicago wanted to be here, and they wouldn't miss their corporate party for ours"

The chatter faded into the background when Susan approached. He managed to tear his gaze from her to notice that her two friends were identical twins, blonde, and in designer clothing. He couldn't look away from the smile Susan wore when she saw him, though.

"I so sorry we're late." She and her friends joined him on the sidewalk. "This is Olivia, and Rissa."

He gave the women a nod, noting their hesitation and traces of discomfort when they looked him in the eye. When he spent too much time with people who knew him, he forgot how strangers reacted to the scar. Thankfully or otherwise, times like this reminded him.

"And this is Andrew," Susan said.

Rissa's attitude shifted in an instant. Knowing he was the guy with the wallet had that effect sometimes. "Andrew Newton?" She shook his hand. "I've heard so much about you." She slid between him and Susan, and pressed close.

He didn't care what she'd heard that caused the change in attitude; he wasn't interested. "Nice to meet you both." He moved around her, to join Susan. "Should we head inside?" He ignored the huff from behind when he wrapped an arm around Susan's waist and guided her to the door.

The brush-off seemed to destroy Rissa's interest.

"Catch up with us later?" Olivia asked.

Susan nodded, and her friends melted into the crowd.

"Your friends seem… nice." He tried to grasp a better word but couldn't find one.

"Olivia is amazing. My link to sanity. Rissa isn't a friend. She does think I'm hilarious."

"Why is that?" Andrew regretted the question as soon as he saw Susan's scowl.

"Because *what kind of repressed prude can't even get a pity fuck by the time she's twenty-one?*"

The venom and mocking in her voice surprised

him as much as the language did. "I don't understand," he said.

She pursed her lips. "It's not like I've taken myself off the market. The opportunity hasn't presented itself."

"I didn't mean you. Your reasons are your own. No judgment. I don't understand her. Why does she care if or when anyone else is fucking? It's not like getting laid is a contest."

"It is, in some videos." Her irritation melted into a shy smile.

"You got me there. Take it from someone who knows—you don't want real life to be a reflection of porn."

Her smile grew, and any follow-up evaporated. He had a growing list of things that made her genuinely happy.

"Come on." She looped her arm through his. "I'll introduce you to some of the gang."

He moved with her from one group to the next, meeting people and hearing more names than he could ever possibly remember. He ran out of obnoxious nicknames after the first four packs. With each new cluster of people, the amusement and gleam in Susan's eyes faded a little more, and her smile resembled a painted-on disguise.

The longer they mingled, the more it sank in— she wasn't afraid of performing; she'd been doing it so long under someone else's definition that she didn't enjoy it. Her smile stayed intact. She shook hands and exchanged hugs and made all the right small talk. But her smile stopped reaching her eyes, and her voice was missing the lilt it got when she was excited.

She didn't need help overcoming deep-rooted stage fright. She needed to learn how to put on a show for herself, and not for whoever she thought might or might not be watching. And God damn, if the notion of a private show for her pleasure didn't fill his head with all sorts of vivid voyeuristic fantasies.

"*Jodie.*" Susan's exclamation jarred Andrew back to the now. She tugged him toward a woman near the far end of the restaurant. "So excited for you."

"Thanks." Jodie was beaming, and as he and Susan approached, she gave them her full attention. "Who's your date?"

Andrew shook her hand. "Resident boy toy."

"He's not," Susan said quickly. "He's just a friend. This is Andrew."

Jodie raised her brows. "Okay…"

"She's being modest. Doesn't tell her boy toy much, though, so I want to hear it from you. What are you pursuing at Stanford?" Andrew kept his tone light and teasing.

Jodie's pleased expression grew, her eyes lighting up. "This is the next step on my way to medical school. There's an advisor at Stanford who's published several papers on prosthetics and transplants, and I get to work with him."

"Tell him what kind." Susan had that impish look that said she knew the punchline.

"Penile."

Andrew was tempted to take the bait, but not if she expected it. Besides, the joke was too obvious. "I've read about that. They're hoping to initially use the science to help vets who lost vital parts in combat, and in the future possibly extend the use to the trans community and other people who can benefit."

"Exactly," Jodie said. "So many people giggle and smirk when I tell them I'm studying penises, but there's a real call for the research."

Susan looked at Andrew, mouth twisted.

"What?" he asked.

"You're not going to ask her to hook up some of your actors?"

He didn't know if he was pleased or disappointed she had him pegged so completely. "First of all—my actors know how to use their assets regardless of size. And second—would it make you feel better if I did?"

"It might. Then I'd know you were you, and not some... I don't know... *not-evil twin* you never mentioned." Susan's tone was playful. At ease.

He liked this side of her. "The word you're looking for is *good*, and I'm the best there is."

"You two are hilarious together." Jodie laughed.

Andrew reached into his wallet and pulled out a business card. "Back to the more serious, just for a minute. I have a friend, Ginny—a dancer—who's starting her residency soon. She's studying in the same field and knows people in the south-east. If you ever want an introduction, drop me a line."

"Yeah. Right. Like you'll remember meeting me in a year or two." Despite Jodie's sarcasm, she took the card.

"I'm serious. And I don't forget people. Especially Suzie-Q's friends. Besides, this isn't the kind of offer I extend to anyone."

"Thank you." She slid the card into her handbag, next to her phone. "Speaking of dancers—do you know her, Susan?"

"She's not that kind of dancer," Andrew said.

Jodie frowned. "I don't understand."

"Ginny takes a lot more clothing off when she's working."

"And probably makes a lot more money doing it," Susan added.

Andrew winked. "Jealous?"

"I may be. You'll introduce me too, won't you?" Despite the topic, Susan looked more at ease than he was used to. She was comfortable with Jodie, as compared to how she acted with the rest of the people here.

"I'll think about it." He turned to Jodie again. "J-Doll, pleasure to meet you."

"Same." Jodie said her goodbyes to both, and apologized for needing to give other guests her attention.

It didn't take long for Susan's attention to drift toward the door.

"Are you okay?" Andrew asked.

"I need some air. If you don't mind."

He remembered the wedding and finding her outside, enjoying the quiet after a few hours of socializing. "We can go, if you're ready." There was no point in pushing her to perform here. She was going to do what she thought her friends wanted, regardless of his prompting. He wasn't in the mood for a battle of wills.

They made their way to the sidewalk, where the traffic had calmed. "It's not that I don't like parties or people," she said. "I adore Jodie and Olivia, but… I don't know. I can't explain it."

He could, and he liked that he understood. "You can only keep up the façade for so long?"

"That's a good way to put it. I can party all night if I don't have to watch myself."

Inspiration struck. "Let's go do that."

"Do…?"

"Party in a place where no one has any expectations of you and you'll never see any of them again."

"I— What?"

He steered her toward the Aror Tech gathering. "Let's crash a party."

SICK TENSION SPILLED through Susan at the suggestion. She didn't know how walking into a place they weren't invited was supposed to help her relax. A *no* hovered on the tip of her tongue, and her brain begged her to pull away. Andrew wrapped his arm around her waist, and the fact that he didn't let go of her for more than a few minutes at a time since she arrived helped beat back the apprehension.

Remembering how mad she was at herself on Sunday, for telling him *no*, was the catalyst she needed, to join him inside. He strolled into the banquet hall without hesitation, smiling and nodding at the few heads that turned in his direction.

A man in a sweater and slacks approached. "Hi. Can I help you?"

They were screwed. So much for that idea. Anxiety coiled inside Susan, threatening to snap.

"I hope so. I'm Andrew, from the Chicago office." Andrew extended his hand. "This is Susan. She's a corporate trainer. Our flight came in late, or we would have been on time."

"Right. Of course. I'm Matt with Human Resources." He shook Andrew's hand. "What department did you say you were with?"

This wasn't so bad. Could they get away with it?

"This is awkward. I'm not supposed to say." Andrew grimaced.

What was he doing? He was going to pick *now* to fail to bullshit someone?

"Right." Matt's voice dropped in volume, and he leaned in. "Most of them don't know we let a lot of Art go recently. You're replacing the director, aren't you?"

Andrew shrugged. "Your words, not mine."

"Of course. Go ahead and mingle. Dinner starts soon. It's great to have you both here."

"What is this?" Susan whispered as soon as Matt was out of earshot.

Andrew dipped his head toward hers, his voice low and his breath hot on her cheek. "According to what I overheard, it's the ArorTech holiday party. They recently bought out a smaller company here."

"HealthLink. Dad's firm brokered the new building deal."

"You already know as much as I do. Still want to do this?"

Pretend she was from a place she'd only been once, worked for a company she knew the barest details about, and did a job she never held—being whoever she wanted, as long as it fell within those guidelines. It was a stupid, terrifying, fascinating idea. "I'm in."

She and Andrew wove through the pockets of people, building on each other's stories as they went.

"I started in photography, but I had grander aspirations," Andrew told one couple who asked how he got into his line of work.

Someone else wanted to get Susan's input on the corporate training programs and what they should expect. She slid into a response without hesitation. "It's always hard to say with a new satellite group. We have standardized materials, of course, but each office needs a unique approach. I did a class in Dallas, where I had them all dance to salsa music."

If she put the right kind of thought into her answers, she could keep them vague with mostly-truths, and people drew their own conclusions. It felt weird, making up stories. At the same time, she was more herself than she ever got to be at Dad's office parties.

"Are the two of you... *you know?*" Another colleague asked.

"A thing?" Andrew filled in the blank.

The man looked like he was anxious for a little bit of corporate gossip. "Well, yeah."

Andrew shook his head. "I find the moment that a woman makes friends with me, she becomes jealous, exacting, suspicious, and a damned nuisance. And I find the moment that I make friends with a woman, I become selfish and tyrannical. So here I am—a confirmed old bachelor and likely to remain so."

She might have been confused by the convoluted response, but the word-for-word recital from *My Fair Lady* and the fact Gossip-Guy seemed impressed were entertaining.

Two hours later, when they finally said their goodbyes and headed outside, she was grinning like she hadn't in ages. How could one evening of lies feel more natural than a night with a people who called her *friend*?

Because despite her fake backstory, she never once had to lie about how she was feeling or mask over basic questions about her. The realization thrilled her.

TWELVE

Susan whirled and laughed, and an unfamiliar pang echoed in Andrew. He couldn't pull his gaze from her. She stopped, facing him, grin wide and eyes sparkling. "That was so much fun. I can't believe… Anyway. Thank you."

"For what?"

"The idea. Bringing me along. I don't know. Tonight." She threw her arms around his neck in a big hug and pressed her warm body to his, chasing away the chill and drawing heat to the surface.

Her tits against his chest. Her breath on his neck. The scent of vanilla and sugar that drilled into his senses.

The hammer of her heart against his ribs—how could he feel that?

Her laughter faded, and she pulled back to meet his gaze. Jesus, she had gorgeous eyes.

He felt her skin against his palm before he realized he was cupping her cheek. When he dipped his head toward hers, her eyes grew wide, and then the lids fluttered closed. He kissed her, and a jolt sped through him, singeing his skin, burning his veins, and making him crave more.

He needed to break away, but she parted her lips in a silent gasp, and he took the invitation, diving his tongue into her mouth to dance and explore.

The way she molded to him chased away sensibility. He drew his hand to the back of her head, to grasp the short hair and hold her captive. She tasted like he expected—innocence and trouble, wrapped together. He didn't want to fuck her; he wanted to strip her down a piece of clothing at a time, and take hours exploring her body and finding out what made her moan, scream, and whimper.

Time to stop. He fumbled to find scant threads of reason and put more than a foot between him and her. He gave Susan a too-bright smile. "Oops."

Her cheerful expression faded into disappointment, before returning half-force. "Don't worry. I won't hold it against you." Her voice was flat.

"Appreciate it, Suzie-Q." It took restraint to grin and act as if he didn't care. It took more, to not tug her back and continue kissing her. What the fuck was wrong with him? He was acting like a horny teenager. It was a kiss. Tempting. Delicious. Soft—

"So… Yeah." She fiddled with the button on her coat sleeve. "It never happened."

"We should go."

She stood in his path, unmoving. "Do you have someplace you need to be?"

He did. He needed to get back to his hotel, jerk off until he was raw, and put this moment behind him. "No. My night is open."

"Can we stay here a little longer? No-expecta-tions-I-promise. I don't want to go home yet. Or you can drop me at Mercy's if that's better for you. I have a key."

The name and plea helped him hang on to reason. When he and Mercy were bumming around the world, she both loathed the idea of going home again, and missed it so much that it kept her up at night, sobbing with homesickness. He nodded toward the sidewalk. "Do you want to walk?"

"Walking sounds good." Susan fell into step beside him, hands jammed in her pockets and gaze cast at her feet.

He mimicked her posture, not trusting his hands to be anywhere else. "What you did inside? Falling into the role and playing that part? That's all you need to do on stage." There. He brought the topic back to the only reason they were spending so much time together. *Good job, me.*

"It's not that easy."

"Why not?"

She jerked her head back toward the restaurant. "Those people don't know me."

"Neither do the people watching you on stage."

"Not all of them, but some do. Family will come to watch. If I'm good at it, eventually people will show up to see *me* dance."

"You're not hearing me." As someone walked past them from the opposite direction, Andrew drifted closer to her. He didn't move away again when the sidewalk was clear. "They know your name. They don't know *you*. They can't say why you use the R&T photography room for practice. They don't know how you take your coffee."

Her arm brushed his, and she stayed close. "That's semantics."

"But it's not." This was the conversation he should have had with her on Sunday, instead of tucking his tail between his legs and running because he couldn't get his libido under control. "Why didn't you want to dance at The Gateway? I'm not judging. No accusation. I want to know."

"Because it was embarrassing." She tucked in her shoulders and moved farther from him.

"But the party wasn't?"

"It's different."

He leaned into her and nudged her toward a coffee shop they were drawing up on. When they stepped inside, warm air bit into the half of his face he could feel, stinging until his skin adjusted to the temperature.

Susan didn't unfold, but she did follow him to the counter.

The girl behind the register—Meg, according to her nametag—glanced at him with a frown, then turned her attention to the register and refused to make eye contact. "What can I get you?" she asked.

On a different night, he'd ask if the scars turned her off or if she was simply less than friendly. His mood would determine if he kept the question to himself or shared it with her. Tonight, Susan's company was too compelling to let him be distracted. "A large coffee, and a small non-fat latte, double shot of sugar-free vanilla."

"How—" Susan snapped her mouth shut when he looked at her.

The cashier took his money and handed over their drinks a moment later, and they found a table near the front window. He slid the latte to Susan. "Lucky guess," he said.

"Thank you." She seemed content to hide behind the cup or her hand or whatever was convenient.

He waited until she put her drink down, then reached over to pin her wrists to the table. He was grateful for the layers of clothing that kept him from touching bare skin. He was also definitely losing his shit if naked wrists were a temptation. "People are always going to have an opinion about you. Pumpkin Spice, over there?" He nodded at Meg. "Odds are as good that my face puts her on edge as they are that she'll forget about us the moment we walk out the door."

"I don't—"

"Hang on." He gave one of Susan's arms a gentle squeeze. "What she thinks? It's not your responsibility. What a random stranger at The Gateway wants to believe? That's not up to you. You said you want to teach dance more than anything. *That's* up to you."

She pulled one hand from his grasp, to take a drink, but didn't extract the other. "Which is all all pretty and simple in theory. It doesn't work that way in practice. Not all of us can shut off caring what other people think about us. We can't all be you."

Her words hurt more than he wanted. Ironic, given the conversation. "Is that what you see in me? Someone who doesn't care?"

"No. Maybe. It's like sometimes I think you do, but others... Don't listen to me. I don't know you."

Let's change that. He stashed the errant thought. "I care about what people think. And not only Mercy. Or you." *Shut up.* "But I learned a long time ago that, if *I* don't think my opinion matters, no one else will."

She drummed her fingers on the table. Great.

Now he'd irritated her. "I hear it, but I don't know how to *do* that." She didn't *sound* annoyed. She bobbed her head back and forth. It was subtle, but it matched the beat spilling from the speakers.

He stood and offered his hand. "May I have this dance?"

She stared at him, bottom lip caught between her teeth. The silence dragged out between them. He didn't know why he was doing this again, after her reaction last time. A tiny voice whispered this was about more than pushing her boundaries; it was personal.

He refused to listen. "No one else is in here but us and Pumpkin Spice." He kept his voice low, so only Susan would hear him.

The corners of her mouth twitched up, but she didn't show any other sign of movement.

SUSAN WASN'T GOING to make the same mistake she did last time. Swallowing the apprehension sprinting through her, she took Andrew's hand and let him pull her to her feet. When he twirled her, she gave an embarrassed laugh. When he pulled her close, her breath caught. She kick-started her heart and forced herself to stay calm, despite the memory of his kiss lingering on her lips. This would be easier if she focused on the fact that he couldn't keep a beat.

She looked at the counter, then ducked her head at the cashier's expression. "She's scowling."

"Who? Pumpkin Spice?" Andrew kept going in what Susan thought might be a weak waltz. Or a two-step. Or a slow-version of a dance-club spaz-out.

If Susan kept her attention on the way his hands felt, one gripping hers and the other at her waist, it was easier to block the urge to hide. "Why are you calling her that?"

"I assume Meg is short for Nutmeg. Makes sense, doesn't it? She works in a coffee shop. She looks like Bratty Spice. One plus one equals Pumpkin."

Susan buried her face in his shoulder. "You're sure it's not because you've got a food fetish?" She should be hesitating to ask the question, but it felt natural.

"I've fetishized a lot of things in my life, but food's not one of them." He whirled them, then pulled her close again.

She wanted to ask if *she* could be one of them.

"Excuse me. You can't do that in here." Meg's irritation cut through the conversation.

Susan paused, but a nudge from Andrew moved her again. He turned to face the register. "Do what?"

"That."

"Not very clear, but let's say I know what you're talking about. Why not?"

The warmth scorching Susan's cheeks was no longer affection, but she didn't have a desire to ask Andrew to stop.

"You're bothering the other customers." Meg's words faded off when Andrew cast his attention around the room.

"There's no one else in here," he said.

"You need to leave."

Andrew turned back to the table but never took his arm from Susan's waist. "Yes, ma'am." He grabbed Susan's drink and handed it to her, before taking his own. They left the shop. As the door swung shut behind them, he whispered in Susan's ear, "Notice how that didn't kill us?"

"Jury's out on that." Despite the gnawing in her gut and the adrenaline pumping through her at the confrontation, she had to admit she was right. He didn't push Meg once she asked them to leave. No one got hurt. It wasn't so bad. Once Susan convinced all of herself of that, not only her brain, she'd be doing better.

He steered her down the street, holding her close. "Let me know when they reach a verdict."

"I had fun. If she hadn't stopped us, I could have danced all night." She peeked up at him through her lashes, trying to gauge his reaction to her play on their earlier conversation.

He smiled. "And still have begged for more?"

"Depends on the partner. And you are a fan of the classic movies, beyond retro porn."

He glanced at her, smile in place. "You googled *The Green Door*? I hope you liked what you found. And no, not so much a fan, as a four-year drama student in high school. A lot of those musicals are burned into my mind."

"You were in drama? I'm so surprised." She laced teasing with her sarcasm.

"I'm wounded." He sounded anything but. "What's that supposed to mean?"

She hesitated. What if she'd read him wrong? Worse—what if he didn't know he was doing it, and she offended him? Instinct said she'd be okay. "You molded yourself into a community where you got to play a part—or a lot of them—and draw all the attention you could ever possibly want, as someone else."

He slowed his pace but didn't drop his arm from around her waist. He tossed his coffee in a nearby bin. It landed with a heavy *thud*. "Do you think I'm playing a part with you?" His tone was more serious than before. Which meant he didn't shut her out like every other time she tried to chip away at his exterior.

She pushed forward. "Are you going to argue you're not? You said earlier my audience doesn't know me. You don't either, the same way I don't know you. Despite your stories."

"What do you want to know?" He sat on a bench and tugged her down next to him. Sincerity shone in his eyes when he looked at her.

She hadn't expected a chance to actually ask. "Are you still in love with Mercy?" The question rolled out before she could consider it.

"No." He didn't flinch.

"If you're not going to be honest with me, there's no point."

"Correction—if you're not going to take me at my word when I *am* being honest, there's no point."

She didn't want to argue. This was her chance to uncover the enigma that was Andrew. If that meant saving the question about her sister for another time, she could do that. "All right. Give me another question?"

"As many as you want."

"When did you decide to stop performing and start watching?"

He gave a shaky laugh and stared at the bench. "You do ask the tough questions, don't you?"

"Should I let you do the asking?" So much for stripping away the mask.

"Hmm… I'm going to take your very generous offer to let me change the subject. What do I want to know?"

She expected him to make her blush, and braced herself to hide the reaction.

"Why blue?" He trailed his fingers through her hair.

The tender gesture caught her off guard and snatched away her thoughts. *Lean in. Kiss him again.* She ignored the impulse. "I wanted hot pink, but the girl who does my hair didn't have any in stock."

"Lucky for me, I like the blue." He rubbed a lock between his fingers. "What does your dad think you're majoring in? In his mind, what are his college dollars buying?"

"Teaching. Like I told you before."

"You hesitate every time you talk about it. In the car. At Kandace's. What aren't you saying?"

She didn't want to get into this, because he'd take it wrong. On the other hand, skipping the question would make it seem like a big deal, and it wasn't. "He jokes about kicking me out if I pursue dancing as part of the teaching." She made sure to put some laughter in her response.

His scowl was worse than she expected. "*Jokes* about it?"

"He's not serious. He was so hurt over Mercy leaving when she was eighteen, he'd never throw one of us out."

Andrew worked his jaw up and down, and then his frown vanished. "No. I'm sure he wouldn't."

The flat, neutral tone was the same she heard

every time he held back. She'd love to know how to unlock the things he hid. The glimpses she got intrigued her. She could see why he and Mercy were such good friends. When he wasn't wearing the mask, he was sweet and fun. Too bad she didn't know how to get him to leave the mask off.

THIRTEEN

ANDREW WAS GRATEFUL Saturday was almost here, and at the same time he'd yet to figure out what to say to Lucas when the time came. He'd play it by ear, most likely.

He gathered his laptop from his temporary office, so he could work over the weekend, and sent Kandace a text. *You free tonight?*

No. Sorry. Lucas has therapy and then dinner with friends. Her message came back too quickly for his liking, especially given the content.

He twitched his thumb over the screen, not making contact. It was tempting to ask where the therapist's office was, so he could go pull Lucas out and put his foot down over the boy ever going back.

His phone beeped in his hand, startling him. *And I'm not giving you the therapist's info,* his sister texted.

I wasn't going to ask. There went that idea. He

wouldn't mind a bit of friendly company to distract him if Susan was free. As he made his way into the lobby, a familiar voice drifted to his ears. "Dad wanted me to drop these off, so they'll be waiting for Ian Monday morning."

Susan. How convenient.

"I'll make sure they're on his desk," Mindy said.

Andrew rounded the corner, to see the two women chatting, a manila folder on the reception desk between them. Susan's smile grew, her eyes twinkling when she saw him, and a rush of possessiveness flowed through him. He wanted that look to be for him alone more often. He shook aside the random notion.

"Hey." Her greeting was as bright and genuine as her look.

"Ladies." He gave a short bow in Mindy's direction, then turned back to Susan. "Do you have plans tonight?"

Susan raised her brows. "Is this for another *lesson*?"

Of course she was going to ask him that in front of a witness. He'd have to talk to her later about what *Mercy doesn't find out* meant. "Nope. I'm simply looking for a dinner companion."

"Sounds like fun." She caught her bottom lip between her teeth.

That was cute. *And a bad sign.* Odd, errant thought. "When are you free?"

"Now. I was dropping off some paperwork for Dad and then heading home for the night."

It was early for dinner, but he liked the idea of hanging out. "Now it is, then. Have a good weekend, Candy Cane." He waved to the receptionist, and then joined Susan outside. "Anywhere specific you'd like to go?"

"The Bistro is always nice."

"The one at my hotel?"

"Is that where you're staying? Totally forgot." There was a slight pause in her step, before she resumed walking.

It *was* a good restaurant. "The Bistro it is."

SUSAN WAS surprised Andrew couldn't hear her heart hammering against her ribs, and shocked that she managed to keep up her half of a conversation on the drive back to his hotel. Since Tuesday night, she hadn't been able to get him off her mind. Not only the kiss, though that had played on a loop in her head. The text from Rissa on Wednesday, teasing that Susan was friends with a porn kingpin and still couldn't get laid and asking if she was defective, didn't help.

What haunted her the most were his stories. How open he was about sex. The way his just-detailed-enough-to-be-tempting tales kept her company when she was alone with her vibrator. It led her to calculate a plan. It was stupid and insane, and there was no way she expected a chance to act on it, but who better to take her virginity than a guy who seemed completely uninterested in commitment, and knew more about sex than probably anyone? It was a bonus that he was kind and considerate. And on top of all that, he invited her back to his hotel.

"Since we're here, do you mind if I stash my laptop in my room?" he asked as they entered the lobby.

This was going way too smoothly. She swallowed, to keep her anticipation and nervous excitement in check. "No problem. I'll head up with you." She had to pin her arms to her sides to keep from tapping her fingers against her leg on the elevator ride up.

He let them into his room and set the computer bag on a desk near the TV. She had no idea how to do this. What to say. A billion half-formed words jammed into her thoughts at once, none making sense. She closed the distance between them when he turned around, and stared at her in surprise.

"Didn't mean to nearly step on you." He laughed.

She managed a chuckle but couldn't think beyond that. It was now or chicken out forever. She draped her arms around his neck and pressed her lips to his, before she could think herself out of it.

A shock raced through her at the kiss. Apparently her memories of the other night weren't as vivid as she thought. And he was kissing her back. It wasn't only that he knew what he was doing—dropping his hands to her hips and nipping at her bottom lip—there was also a feeling to it she couldn't describe, but that left her craving more. Lord, this was amazing.

He dug his fingers into her skin, gripping tight, and she pressed closer. Her heart hammered in her ears, and his erection dug into her stomach. She whimpered against his mouth, unable to think about anything but how good this felt and what came next. Would it hurt? She didn't care, if it was wrapped in this kind of intensity.

He shoved her back to arm's length, let go, and put a couple more feet between them. "What the fuck?" His gravelly question was breathless.

Not quite the response she hoped for. "I was thinking... sex?" That was less than intelligent. She struggled to make her brain work again. Despite his question, he didn't look angry. She'd seen the expression before, though. The first time he watched her dance, at R&T. The other night when they kissed. Lust? That had to be it.

"Whatever I've said, I've obviously given you the wrong impression about our relationship."

She frowned. "I thought we were friends. You invited me to dinner for company. We enjoy hanging out."

"We are," he said. "I adore spending time with you, Suzie-Q."

"I'm not asking you to be my boyfriend. I'm tired of being a virgin. Friends help each other out, don't they? It's not like I'm saving myself for marriage."

"Which—good on you. But I'm not the guy you want to do this with."

The rejection stung more than she expected, burrowing through her chest and into her gut. "Why not?" She tried not to let the hurt worm its way into her voice. "There's attraction. You know what you're doing. It's because of me, isn't it? I'm too inexperienced." She should have considered that. Of course he wasn't interested in someone who had no idea what they were doing. It was a selfish request.

He closed the distance between them, gripped her shoulders, and guided her to the edge of the bed. Then he pulled a chair from the desk, placed it as far back from her as the room allowed, and sat. "You don't want *this* to be your first time." Great. Now he sounded like he pitied her. "It doesn't matter if you're *saving yourself* or not. An intense experience like this, especially if it's done right, will make you feel an emotional connection. You need a guy you already have that with. Even if you decide you're okay with casual sex down the line, don't make it a starting point."

The condescension hurt as much as the rejection, and venom bubbled inside before she could stop it. "You're not worried about me getting attached. You're scared of what Mercy will say if she finds out." She wanted to take the words back before he furrowed his brows, but she couldn't find the strength to do so.

"For someone who wants to outgrow her sister's shadow, you sure do talk about her a lot."

Susan had steered the conversation down a lane she didn't want it drifting anywhere near. And that didn't stop her from hopping on for the ride. She was too hurt to let this go the way she needed to. "If I were more like her, would you tell me *yes*? I know you never got over her."

"I'm going to tell you this once, and if you mention it again, it will probably be the last time we speak. I'm not fucking in love with Mercy." He ground out each word separately through gritted teeth

Her brain screamed at her to shut up, but her heart kept moving her lips. "Really? What would you call this intense devotion then?"

"I call it devotion. I owe her my life."

"*Wow*. That's melodramatic. You're right—that's not love. It's obsession."

"You've got a lot of opinions about a world you don't understand."

"I'm trying to learn, and I keep getting cock-blocked by people who think they know what's best for me." Frustration slid into her voice and clenched her lungs.

"So stop listening to them and do what *you* think is best for you."

She wanted to scream incoherently. Let out a long roar until her throat was raw and her ears ached. "You're one of them."

And like that, his anger vanished behind a blank slate. "Consent goes both ways." His tone was cool and completely infuriating.

"You didn't say, *no, I don't want to have sex with you.* You fed me a bullcrap line about how this was for my own good." Why couldn't she be as chill about this as he was? Every time she opened her mouth, she made a bigger fool of herself.

"And you didn't believe me, so I'm changing my answer. If you don't like the opinions of those around you, walk away."

"Like Mercy did?" Where the hell did that come from? Right. From years of resentment at her sister, for abandoning the family to go have fun.

"That's not—"

"I'm not interested in leaving the people I care about and who care about me, to explore the world. There's so much for me to learn *here*. The world can wait until I have my friends by my side."

"This has been eating at you for a while."

"Damn it. *Stop*. Don't be calm. Or rational. Or condescending. Do you feel?" She clenched her jaw, to keep more words from tumbling out, and forced herself to count to ten. When he didn't interrupt, she tried to sound more reasonable. "She walked out of the house with barely more than a *goodbye*, and left her family and friends behind because... why? She wanted to go screw guys in other countries?"

Andrew's chuckle sounded bitter. "Is that the version your father told you? He kicked her out. Disowned her. Your brothers refused to talk to her. He told her there would be consequences if she reached out to you. He cut her off from the entire family."

That wasn't right. Dad would never. "He was so upset about her being gone."

"Because her choice was to conform or leave, and she chose to leave. It's the same choice he's about to give you. She didn't abandon her friends. She never lost contact with Liz, and I spent countless nights listening to her sob because she couldn't go back home."

Righteous indignation soured to doubt and churned inside with embarrassment, until Susan was sure she was going to be sick. "He welcomed her back. He's been happy to have her around again. Once she accepted the olive branch he extended…" Was that true?

"I don't know the man." Andrew stared at his clasped hands. "He's softened, or she exaggerated, or he thinks she's respectable now that she's with Ian. I can only tell you what she told me. But I trust her, and her pain at being cut out of your lives always seemed real."

"Then he's changed." This wasn't only about how upset Susan had been at Mercy for leaving. If this was true, it was possible Dad would do the same to her. She couldn't believe that. "Losing her made him see he was wrong. He won't make that mistake again." He wouldn't actually kick Susan out for pursuing dancing.

Andrew shrugged. "Like I said, I don't know him. My opinion is you can't assume he's bluffing. You grew up with him, though."

"So you're saying I should quit?" How did they go from her wanting to lose her virginity to Andrew suggesting she give up her passion?

"*No.* Jesus Christ, nothing like that." He met her gaze, intensity burning in his dark eyes. "You should pursue this for all you're worth. I wouldn't be helping you if I didn't see a gift in you that deserves to be nurtured. You're brilliant when you let go. I'm saying you can't assume your dad is joking. I'm sorry." He said the last bit so quietly, she wasn't sure she heard right.

"I can't give up my family."

"If you really want to do this dancing thing— teaching, performing... If that's what drives you? You can't give that up either. If you walk away, you'll always regret it, and regret makes people hateful and hard."

Indecision built inside, threatening to tear her heart in half. Susan had never felt this kind of intensity before, and she wanted to rip it out and stomp on it, to make it go away. "If I walk away from the people I love, I'll regret it."

"Do you want to know how Mercy saved my life?" Andrew asked.

That was the last thing she needed. "I'm not up for a story that's glamor and glitz, wrapped in the kind of sex you think I'm too fragile to handle. Especially if it involves Mercy."

"This story is anything but glamorous. There's no sex, and I promise it comes back to you."

FOURTEEN

Andrew couldn't believe he offered to tell her this story. Ten minutes ago, he was berating himself for turning Susan down, arguing that he wouldn't have hesitated if she were anyone else. He didn't know if that was because of her or Mercy, but a tiny nagging voice said it had more to do with Susan.

Now he was volunteering to spill a past that haunted him six years after the fact, and about which only he and Mercy knew the entire truth.

Susan stared at him, jaw clenched and eyes rimmed with red.

He needed whatever resolve she had, to make it through this. He summoned a light tone. "It was a couple of weeks before Christmas, and I was in Belgium. I was twenty-two, and it had been a few years since I traveled alone. We made a lot of friends out there, and we all tended to drift together and apart, depending on where impulse took us."

"That's nice?" Susan twisted her mouth.

"Stay with me. There's a point to this."

"I'm not going anywhere."

Her sincerity sank into him, and despite her expression, he had no doubt she was staying right here and wasn't upset about it. He cleared his throat. "Anyway. I was shacked up with a woman I met in the red-light district. She knew exactly who I was. I was paying her for pictures, the sex was decent, and she let me crash on her couch. She was sweet. Hid it from her johns..." The past surged forward in a haze of pain and regret, and he stammered. This was going to be harder to talk about than he thought. "I was also kind of a warning to her ex-boyfriend that she moved on."

"So you've always been a rescue-the-maiden-in-distress kind of guy?" Susan asked. She leaned in, listening attentively. That made things worse.

"Yeah, well... not this time. I've had a lot of vices over time. Back then, they were alcohol and GHB." Jesus this hurt. "One night we drank, we got high, we passed out. Like pretty much every night. Her asshole ex-boyfriend lit her trailer on fire with us in it. We both slept through it. I sustained third-degree burns." The memory surged inside, scorching with agony. "She died."

"Oh my gosh. I'm so sorry."

He forced a smile. The tough part of the story was yet to come. "Me too. I spent weeks in the hospital, wrapped in bandages, writhing in pain and loathing myself. Because I didn't protect her. Because I ached. Because I was jealous she didn't have to live with the scars, when I did. That last one made me hate myself the most."

Susan opened her mouth, and he held up a hand to silence her. If she interrupted now, he wouldn't be able to finish. "Mercy found me about a month later. She apparently called every hospital and local police station, until she tracked me down. At the time, I hated her for doing it. Which made me loathe myself more. You see the cycle. She walked into my hospital room the day I planned to kill myself."

"Fuck me." Susan's whisper barely reached his ears.

He was grateful she wasn't spewing false pity. That was the one thing he didn't need. "She was sympathetic. Kind. Exactly what one would expect. Tried to feed me bullshit lines, like it wasn't my fault, and reminded me I tried to be there for the woman. The whole time Mercy was talking, I was trying to figure out how to tell her *goodbye* without cluing her into my plan.

"Then she said something. I don't remember what, but it was one of those obligatory things people say to those who survived. It struck me hard, and it felt insincere—so unlike Mercy. I snapped. I shouted at her, *Because everything happens for a reason? She'd want me to go on with my life? Blah blah—fuck you, too?*"

He breathed deep, to stem the flow of emotion that came with the memory, but it didn't help. "She stared at me and didn't say anything for the longest time. I wondered if she was going to walk out, and I wanted her to, so I'd have another reason to hate myself. Then she told me shit happens all the time for no other reason than people suck. As for what my prostitute friend wanted, my life should be about what I wanted. If I wanted to keep living, I would. If not, that was on me. I couldn't shift that blame to anyone else."

"I can't believe… What did you do?"

"I told her to get out and that I never wanted to see her again, and while we were at it, what the fuck was wrong with her? She was the worst fucking grief counselor ever. She pointed out she wasn't a counselor; she was my friend, and we were always honest with each other. I disagreed. It was the perfect reason. The truth hurt, and I wanted a little fantasy in my life. And why the fuck hadn't she left yet? She looked wounded, but she said *goodbye* and walked out."

"Then what?" Susan's voice cracked.

"I seethed. I hated myself, and then I hated her. At least the cycle had changed. Why didn't she try harder to tell me how amazing and wonderful life was? She didn't bother feeding me lines I didn't want to hear. Night crept into morning, and I realized she was right. If I stayed in this world for anyone besides me, I wouldn't be happy. I called her, begged her to come back, and told her I owed her an apology. She said I didn't owe her anything. And she stayed by my side until they released me." The skin grafts covered most of the damage, but he knew what lay underneath.

"Wow."

He needed to numb the memory. Too bad he also quit drinking back then. "My point is, if you keep dancing, do it because you're passionate about it. Mercy wanted her freedom. I wanted my future. You want your expression. Family expectations are a bad reason to throw away your dreams. Same goes for the sex. Don't do it because you're tired of not doing it. Do it because you want to."

She gave him a half-smile. "You sure know how to make a point."

"That's why I'm in porn, Suzie-Q." He couldn't linger in the hurt any longer. She leaned forward and kissed him on his scarred cheek. Though he didn't have nerves there, he swore it burned.

"I can't believe you're comparing deciding to live to whether or not I should keep dancing," she said.

"It's my understanding that when you're

passionate about anything, giving it up is a bit like dying."

She shifted on the mattress, scooting back to pull her legs under her. "So what are you passionate about?"

"Besides living every day to its fullest?"

"That's actually pretty good."

Fuck it. If he was dragging skeletons out of his closet, he might as well go for broke. "Lucas."

"Your nephew?"

"He's my son." Andrew gave her the Cliffs Notes version of finding out he was a dad when he was eighteen, and his reasons for both leaving Lucas with Kandace and wanting that to change now. He left out the conversion therapy information. There was only so much pain he could take in an evening.

Susan fiddled with a loose thread on the comforter. "Now I feel childish and immature, carrying on like I did, given what you're going through."

"Don't," he said quickly. "My reasons for not sleeping with you have a teensy tiny bit to do with Mercy, but a whole lot more to do with me enjoying your company. I respect you. I'm choosing friend-ship over sex."

"So if you couldn't stand me?" A hint of teasing lay under her question.

It was nice to slide into the joking. "All other things being equal? I'd fuck the hell out of you."

"Then damn me, for being sweet."

"Damn you to hell." With the story fading, he could breathe again. It left raw bits inside, but those would ice over with time. "Did you still want The Bistro for dinner?"

"Or you take me back to my car?"

"Only if you want to leave. Otherwise, we order room service and see what's on HBO, while I find out what skeletons you've got in *your* closet."

She patted the bed next to her. "Only if you join me over here. I promise to behave and keep my hands to myself."

"Give up a secret first." He tried to keep his tone light.

"Um…" She screwed up her face. "When I was seventeen, I lied about my age, in order to audition as a Jazz cheerleader."

He moved to sit next to her on the bed and grabbed the room service menu in the process. "That needs a lot more embellishment. Pick what you want for dinner, and we'll work on adding a little flair to your story." If he kept this up a little longer, he could stuff the past back in its box—that was the plan. Having her here was numbing old wounds, and that was a good start.

FIFTEEN

"I WAS THINKING... SEX?" SUSAN MOLDED HER BODY to Andrew's, and he swore he felt her skin through his shirt.

He dragged his fingers up her bare back, memorizing how soft her naked body was against his palms. He didn't remember how her clothes came off, but he wasn't complaining. "I was thinking you're brilliant." He kissed along her neck, burning her sweet scent into his mind.

She gasped and squirmed against him with each new touch. When she reached for the hem of his shirt, he pushed her hands away. Her pout made his rigid cock ache with the need to thrust between those full lips. "Why not?" she asked.

He didn't know. Couldn't put it into words. "Because I said so." He nipped at her skin and moved one hand to her breast. *We're not going to do this*. The faint voice nudged the back of his mind. Apparently, they were. She was willing. So was he. No reason to stop now.

He wanted to memorize every detail of her body. Where her freckles were. The color of the nipple he tweaked and pulled, to elicit a delicious series of sighs. None of it stuck in his mind, except her voice and intoxicating smell. They would have to do. He lowered his head and dragged his tongue along the hard nub. She gasped and pushed into his mouth, writhing under his touch.

He continued to suck and lick, while he glided his hand down her stomach and between her legs. Fuck, she was slippery. He wanted to prolong this— make her come over and over—but he wanted to be inside her more. He found her clit, swollen between her folds, and traced circles around her tender button. She ground against his touch, squirming and moaning. When she drew her nails up his back, he felt the sharp sting on one side, but not the other. That didn't make any sense; the scars didn't run that far.

He expected screams when she came, but her whimpers weren't bad either. She fumbled with his zipper, and he helped her slide it down. Time slowed as each tooth separated, humming in his head. Buzzing. Taunting him.

That wasn't a zipper. What was it?

He didn't care. He wanted to feel her cool

fingers around his shaft. Wanted to slide inside her soaking pussy. Stretch her out.

His eyes flew open, and it took a few seconds for him to make sense of the dark hotel room. The hammer of his pulse in his ears drowned out any other sound. He struggled to process his surroundings. *Fucking dream.* He was surprised he didn't wake up humping the bed, as turned on as he was.

The rest of the world swam into focus, as consciousness set in. Susan lay on the other half of the mattress, curled around a spare pillow and sleeping soundly. Great. They fell asleep talking, clothes on, about as far apart from each other as possible, while still being in the same bed.

He hadn't told her the complete truth about why he wouldn't have sex with her, but what he said was mostly accurate. It wasn't simply about wanting to keep her friendship or not wanting her to get attached. If he crossed that line with her, he'd have a hard time letting go. She wasn't going to be happy with a guy who was so far from wanting a commitment, it wasn't funny. Considering most things were funny in the right light…

And staring at her, thinking about sex— including why they weren't having it—didn't make his hard-on go away.

Careful not to wake her, he extracted himself from the bed and stumbled into the bathroom. He didn't turn on any lights. Didn't want to disturb

Susan or see confirmation in the mirror that he wore a pained, haunted look. He splashed cold water on his face. Instead of chasing away the lingering traces of the dream, it froze the images in his head, making them vivid.

His dick strained against his jeans, aching and relentless. What was he doing? This wasn't him. He either went after the girl, if he wanted to get laid, or walked away and found a different outlet. He yanked down his zipper, reliving the pressure but not the agony. When he wrapped his hand around the shaft, he had to bite the inside of his cheek, to keep a groan from escaping.

Desperation flooded him while he stroked his cock. The dream superimposed itself on reality, drawing him into the unfinished fantasy until he swore he could feel Susan's tight, wet pussy snug around him, milking and urging. He pressed his free hand to the wall for balance, jerking hard as he fell into the images. How she would feel. The sweet scents of sugar and vanilla. Her soft cries when she climaxed.

He came hard, thrusting his hips, and a spasm rolling through him. He didn't ease up tugging his dick until he was spent and worn out. He took a few minutes to catch his breath, cleaned up the mess on him and the counter, and zipped up again.

The clock near the bed said it was only one in the morning. He wasn't going back to sleep any time soon. Not with her in the room. His phone hummed on the nightstand. That was what had woken him up. He grabbed it and pulled up the text message that arrived half an hour ago.

It was a picture of a blonde, taken from above, with a fantastic view down the front of her dress. She looked familiar. Susan's friend? No. *Friend* wasn't the right word. *Rissa*—that was her name. The note with the selfie read, *Can a girl get a ride?*

How'd you get my number? he asked.

Snagged it from Jodie. Is that a yes?

That was the last time he did someone a favor like pass along a business card. He looked between the photo on his phone and Susan sleeping in his bed. His cock throbbed, already half-hard again.

Fuck this. He needed an outlet. *I wouldn't mind you riding me. Where are you?*

Seconds later, he had an address. He scribbled a short note for Susan, barely aware of what it said. The brightness in the hallway was a shock to his senses. Stepping outside into the parking garage didn't clear his head. He spent the ten-minute drive to the bar pushing the fucking sleeping vision to the back of his mind.

Rissa was waiting outside when he pulled up. He rolled down the passenger window. "Need a lift, gorgeous?"

"I was worried you'd never ask." She bit her

bottom lip—a gesture that looked scripted—and hopped into the SUV. "My place or yours?"

"I'm hoping yours is closer." He let his mouth run on auto-pilot. If his brain took over, he'd be talked out of this before they started.

She laid her hand on his thigh, gliding higher as he drove, until she reached his cock. She drew her nails lightly over denim. "And I thought I was eager." She traced the head of his dick.

"A good picture always gets me started." There was no way he was telling her the erection lingered from the dream and had nothing to do with her. He could convince both of them this was about Rissa if he focused on the now.

"I wouldn't mind you doing a little camera work on me, if you want a memento of tonight."

He hid his cringe. This was worse than an off-the-shelf porn script. It didn't matter. When they got back to her place, he'd bury his face between her legs, making her scream in pleasure, then fuck her until he was spent. It was that simple. She was attractive, she knew what she was getting herself into, and he needed to get laid, so he could start thinking like a reasonable human being again.

She gave directions while she continued to tease him through his jeans, and moments later, he pulled the car into the driveway she indicated. He didn't shut off the engine.

She gave him an exaggerated sultry look. "You're coming inside, aren't you?"

Of course he was. Turn off the ignition. Pocket the keys. Follow that round, bouncy ass through the front door... "Not tonight."

"Do I need to beg? Is that what gets you off?" She scooted as close as the bucket seats allowed.

He nudged her back to her side. "No. Turns out I'm not in the mood after all."

She searched his face, half-smile fading into a scowl. "Limp-dicked asshole." She climbed from the vehicle and slammed the door behind her.

Yeah. That sounded about right. He couldn't pick out a clear thought beyond which direction to drive, as he headed back to the hotel. Now that he was awake, the past hammered in to collide with the present, mocking him with memories of his guilt from the fire, the brief time he and Mercy dated, and the sweet girl up in his room. Sleeping, if she was lucky.

He made his way into the hotel's twenty-four-hour restaurant, took a seat at the bar, and slipped the guy a Benjamin Franklin to leave the bottle of tequila after he poured Andrew a shot. Fuck local liquor laws. Fuck the past. Fuck six years of sobriety. And fuck whatever pathetic imitation of a sense of morals was trying to grow inside.

He stared at the golden liquid and the scarred

bar-top underneath. There was probably a metaphor in there somewhere, but he wasn't interested in looking for it. When he managed to shove Susan out of his head, ghosts of heat and pain seared back to torment him. If he pushed the disaster in Belgium aside, Mercy's voice from seven years ago mocked him. *Is it really that hard for you to imagine monogamy? Are you that fucked up, you can't picture yourself with only one other person for more than half an hour at a time?*

That cycled back to Susan.

"Hey, pal. My shift is up. Can I get you anything else?" The bartender interrupted his stare-down.

Andrew turned a bleary-eyed gaze to his phone. It was almost six-thirty. *Shit.* He had to meet Kandace and Lucas in a couple of hours. At least he hadn't touched the tequila. So much for sleep. His focus was in too many other places, for him to worry about how he was going to tell Lucas about his real parentage—that was one thing to be grateful for. "I'm good. Thanks, man."

He couldn't face Susan, and he could think of one solid way to make sure it wasn't an issue. He sent Mercy a text message. *Hope the honeymoon was lots of naked fun. I know it's early, but Susan is asleep in my hotel room. She probably needs a ride.*

He didn't expect a response this time of day— Mercy and Ian didn't get in until last night—so he was surprised when her reply buzzed through a couple minutes later. *Explain.*

Put the pieces together yourself, he typed.

I asked you for one favor. One.

Guilt wormed its way in, to join the chaos already assaulting his cluttered mind. That was the last thing he needed—another list item to feel bad about. *I'm not that good a guy*, he wrote.

He pocketed the phone, ignoring any other notes from Mercy, and headed back to his car. Kandace would forgive him if he showed up a little early. It was better than staying here.

SIXTEEN

Susan didn't like waking up alone in someone else's hotel room. Last night's revelations lingered in her head and heart. She'd wanted to know what lay under the surface for Andrew, but she never expected so much pain.

As he'd talked, looking like the words caused him agony, she wanted to do something—*anything*—to stop his hurting. A hug and a pat on the back hardly seemed appropriate.

But when he talked about Lucas, pride and adoration shone through the grief.

If she was curious before, she was enthralled now. Would he close off this morning, now he'd slept away reliving the past? She'd find out if she had any idea where he was.

Her gaze fell on a scribbled note. *Stepped out. Back soon.* That didn't give her much to go on. The chime that woke her, a text from Mercy, helped her draw a couple of conclusions but didn't give her any answers.

Do you need a ride? Mercy said.

Susan wasn't going to bother asking how her sister knew. It seemed as though Andrew's definition of *Mercy doesn't find out* was different than Susan's. Something told her this meant no more glimpses of the real Andrew. The realization gnawed at her.

She nearly replied to Mercy with a *no*, but the night before left her with uneasy questions about their family, and this seemed as good a time as any to see if she could get answers. She sent back a simple, *Yes please. I'll be in the lobby.*

She was hurt Andrew left without a word. He did have to see his sister. Maybe she slept through him trying to wake her up. She didn't think that was the case. Apparently a night of sleep was all it took, for his mask to fall back into place.

When Mercy's familiar Honda pulled up outside the hotel, Susan stashed most of her pondering for later and hopped into the passenger seat. So… what *was* the best way to ask, *Was Dad really an asshole to you, or is your best friend exaggerating?*

Mercy navigated the car to the main road. "Are you going home? And are you all right"

"My car's at the office. Your office. And my pride's a little wounded."

"Do you want to talk about it?"

What did Andrew tell her? "My car? Not really. And there's nothing else to talk about, either."

Mercy frowned. "That good, huh?"

"You're going to have to tell me what you expect me to say, because my night was full of surprises, but I suppose none of them are news to you." Susan sighed and slouched in her seat.

Mercy handed over her phone. "I got these. That's all I know."

Susan frowned as she scrolled through a conversation with Andrew. Her gut clenched at his clipped notes and the innuendo behind them. She dropped the device back in its cradle. "It went like this—I threw myself at a guy who feels like he owes you his life, and he said *no*, and then we talked so long, I managed to forget how humiliated I was. And don't you dare smirk."

"I'm not." Mercy adopted a straight face again.

"You should have more faith in him. He's been a perfect gentleman." Well, not completely. But he definitely wasn't trying anything *like that* with Susan any time soon.

Instead of pointing her car down the main highway, toward the R&T offices, Mercy pulled into a coffee shop drive through. It was early, so there was no line. She ordered them drinks with extra espresso, then parked at the edge of the lot. She took a long swallow of coffee before she faced Susan. "I don't know what you talked about, but I owe him as much as he owes me. He doesn't like to admit it. But I also know what he's capable of, and I would cut him out of my life completely, before you had to go through that."

That didn't sound right. "Like what?"

"Andrew doesn't do things like exclusive relationships."

Since when was Mercy such a drama queen? Susan tried to sip her coffee, but it scalded her tongue. She set it in the cup holder. "I'm not dating him. Or sleeping with him—thanks to him, not me. We were hanging out. Why did you leave home when you were eighteen?"

Mercy choked on her drink, and coughed several times before finding her voice. "I wanted to see the world, and life here was oppressive."

"The real reason. Not the bullshit story you tell people, to sound cool."

"God damn. He talks too much." Mercy leaned her head back against the rest and focused on the roof of the car. "Dad kicked me out. Told me he never wanted to see me again. And that I wasn't supposed to talk to you. He didn't need me filling your head with worthless bullshit. His words, by the way, not mine."

Susan didn't know what kind of answer she expected, but the reality chewed an empty pit behind her ribs. Their father wasn't callous like that. "Why didn't you ever tell me?"

"Because Dad adores you. I missed everything about here when I left, and it took me ages to get over the fact that I couldn't talk to the family. Why would I take that from you?"

"I thought… I thought you were being selfish and didn't care. And you never corrected me." She didn't know why this was so easy to accept, while at the same time it ached all the way to her core. It was like someone upended her view of reality, and it sucked, but part of her had been waiting for it to happen.

"Andrew talks big, and he knows when he's embellishing, but he's typically pretty honest about that. Hates Dad for it." Mercy shifted in her seat. "I have a list of four people I'd do anything for—there aren't even enough to make it five. Ian, Liz, Andrew, and you. Dad won't ever be on there, reconciliation or not. But that relationship works for you, and he's been kind since I came back. It's not my place to destroy your time with him."

"I didn't know. I'm so sorry." All these years, the things Susan thought about her sister… \so completely wrong.

"It is what it is. Are you sure you're all right? Whatever happened, you woke up—"

"Alone in a hotel room that wasn't mine. I know. My ego's wounded. I'm good otherwise. Thank you for coming to get me."

Mercy squeezed Susan's knee. "I'm always here

for you. Just don't make me choose between you and Andrew," she said in a teasing tone, complete with wink.

Susan needed to process the morning's revelations, and she didn't know what to think about her father, but the joke made her feel better. "I won't. Cross my heart, hope to die."

"Thanks." Mercy's frown vanished so quickly, Susan wondered if she imagined it.

"I should let you get back. I'm sorry for interrupting your honeymoon."

"Good idea."

The new information raced in Susan's thoughts while Mercy drove. If Dad had changed, there was nothing to worry about. But who would do what he did to Mercy to an otherwise good kid? If it was true, there must be more bad to Mercy than Susan knew, but that didn't feel right either.

Susan knew one thing for sure, out of the entire mess of confusion—Andrew was right. If she didn't pursue her passion, she'd never forgive herself. If she couldn't get past what held her back, and find a way to move forward with the kind of teaching she wanted to do, she'd always wonder why she gave it up.

Before she knew it, the ten-minute journey to her car was over, and Mercy was parking next to it in the lot.

"I have another favor to ask. Do you mind if I

borrow one of the offices here today? I want to make some calls, and it seems more professional here." And there was less of a chance for interruption.

"Of course. Don't stay too late. Set the alarm when you're done. You know the drill," Mercy said.

Susan grabbed her coffee and hopped from the car. "Thank you. For everything."

Mercy looked like she wanted to say something, then smiled and waved. "See ya."

Susan got settled at Reception and logged into the network. When she said she'd done everything she could to get a dance job, it wasn't completely true. She'd been so hung up on landing a high-profile gig—full of glitz, glamor, and with a low rate of acceptance—she avoided the more obvious opportunities. Teaching at smaller, private studios. Performing more often, with less in-the-spotlight groups. If the point was to fill her résumé, she needed to stop being so picky. And if she had to be honest with herself, the appeal of the bigger venues was that they gave her a better excuse when she failed.

She started down the list of studios, phoning and speaking with managers, seeing who was looking, and talking to anyone and everyone who would take her call. After several hours, she had only had one nibble, but she jumped on it. Making the interview meant taking time off work, but it wasn't as though she'd miss the paycheck. She'd tell Dad it was classroom observation, in conjunction with her major. Not *technically* a lie.

She wouldn't keep this from him, but there was no reason to tell him before things were set in stone. When he heard, he'd be happy for her.

And if not... She'd deal with that bridge when she reached it.

———

ANDREW ASKED the waitress to keep the coffee coming, but he didn't know if there were sufficient amounts in the restaurant to ward off the creeping exhaustion. He struggled to focus on breakfast, rather than on how Susan was reacting to what he did. He couldn't explain why he'd texted Mercy or given her the impression he did. However, running on two hours of sleep and some haunted fucking memories and dreams, it seemed like the smartest way to keep himself in check.

"Why didn't you bring your girlfriend?" Lucas's question dragged Andrew back to the meal.

Andrew must have missed a detail somewhere in the conversation. "Who?"

"Susan. The one with the blue hair."

Kandace met Andrew's gaze, then took a sip of her iced tea.

What the hell was that look supposed to mean? "She's a friend," Andrew said.

"Oh." Lucas poked at his waffles and rolled a strawberry around. "One who might come down with you next time?"

Andrew liked the excuse both to visit Lucas again and see Susan. "It's up to her, but I'll ask. How's therapy?" It would have tasted better to ask how the institutionalized brainwashing was going, but he didn't want to argue. Not today. Not with what he was here to say.

Lucas speared the helpless fruit and shoved it in his mouth. He added several others in quick succession.

"Hey. What's up?" Andrew nudged him.

Lucas scowled. "Mom said you wanted to talk me out of it. I don't know why you care."

"Because I *do* care. I worry about you."

"It's fine. I like it a lot. I'm learning about how I shouldn't listen to my hormones because there are more important things in life."

Andrew didn't have a good argument for that. "It's true. Hormones screw with a lot of otherwise rational thoughts."

"But any avenue to make a buck?" Lucas finally looked at him.

This wasn't the worst possible way the conversation could have started, but it was high on the list.

"Hon, Andrew has something he needs to tell

you." Kandace reached across the table and covered Lucas's hand. "Hear him out, for me?"

"I'm listening," Lucas said.

Great. Now their talk was born of obligation. He looked at Kandace.

She gave him a sympathetic smile and turned to Lucas. "You know how I've told you that you're adopted, but I love you as much as any mom loves her son?"

"Yes?" Lucas dragged the word out, making it last several syllables.

"I'm your father." Andrew felt a huge weight lift in saying the words. "Kandace is your aunt, and she took you in when you were born, so you could have a better life."

Lucas gave a choked-off laugh. "That's not funny. Out of all the mean jokes you've ever told, that's the worst." Andrew opened his mouth, but the boy wasn't done yet. "In fact, I don't understand why I'm the one kid who has to have the screwed-up uncle. None of my friends have to deal with relatives who make stupid jokes and try to embarrass them whenever they're around." He looked at Kandace. "Why can't I have a normal, broken, single-parent home, like a normal kid?"

"It's not a joke." Andrew didn't know where to start in processing the statement, let alone responding to it.

Lucas's twisted expression morphed to a frown.

"Then it's a shitty truth. You should have kept your mouth shut, for once." He pushed back from the table. "I'm waiting in the car."

"*Hey.*" Kandace's bark echoed off the walls, drawing stares.

"Don't." Andrew didn't want to embarrass the kid worse if that was part of the issue.

She sank back into her seat. "I'm sorry.

"I shouldn't have done it. You were right. Isn't that fantastic to hear?" Andrew meant to keep his tone casual but didn't succeed.

"Not really. Do you want to talk to him, or should I?"

He waved a waitress over, asked for the check, and handed her his card. "Give him some room to deal. I'll come back down in a few days and spend some real time with him. Thanks for letting me try."

"Talk to you soon." She grabbed her purse and followed the path Lucas took out of the restaurant.

Andrew scrubbed his face and sighed. He'd disappointed his best friend. Most likely pissed off another person he was starting to think of as a good friend. His own son couldn't stand him. If he were someone else, he'd let it send him into a spiral of frustration. Fortunately, he didn't do that. He'd lose himself in work, and everything would be fine.

SEVENTEEN

Andrew didn't get as much work done over the weekend as he planned. Or any at all. He spent the rest of Saturday sleeping. Which meant that night he was up at odd hours. He became familiar with the Cinemax movies of the month and had confirmation that cable porn hadn't changed in ten years.

Now he was back in the R&T offices, he hoped he could focus. A knock on the door drew his attention.

Mercy stood in the doorway. "I wanted to make sure you got what you needed from my staff last week."

"And then some." He could be all business. "I'll be out of here by the end of the week. Probably working from Kandace's. until I leave after Christmas." *If I can make things right with Lucas.* "As always, you rocked it. It works great."

She gave him a small smile and turned to leave. "Glad to hear it."

"Hang on. How was the honeymoon?" Okay, so he couldn't leave things tense between them.

She looked back at him. "Amazing." Her smile turned genuine. She only glowed like that when she talked about Ian. She was lucky she had someone she loved so much, who felt the same about her. Susan deserved the same. *Where the fuck did that come from?*

"I'm glad," he said.

"How was my sister?"

And there it was. Out in the open. A way to remind everyone he was the asshole who needed to keep his distance. He adopted his favorite leer. "Fantastic."

"That's not the way she tells it. She said you couldn't get it up."

He doubted Susan said anything anywhere near that callous, whether or not she told Mercy the truth. "You know how girls like to talk. It's always the guy's fault if she doesn't get off. I wasn't there for her. I wanted to blow my wad and move on." He managed to say it all without flinching.

Mercy closed the door and took a seat across from him. "If you're going to play the pig card, stick to pervy. You've never been selfish."

"Don't know what you're talking about." Why was it so important to him to keep up this façade?

"I know what happened. Susan told me. I want to know why you're spinning it so hard, to make yourself sound like the asshole. If it's about ego, you need to feed your bullshit to someone else."

"Why does it matter to you what did or didn't happen?"

"Really?" She looked at him, brow furrowed. "Because she's my sister."

"And I'm one of your closest friends. Why was it okay for you to slum it with me, but not for her?" Was that why he did this? Mercy's request bothered him? No. He was talking circles around the issue. Pushing for the sake of argument.

"So this is an object lesson of some sort? You haven't convinced me I was wrong to make the request."

He leaned in, to rest his forearms on the desk. "But you don't believe anything happened."

"Susan tells me nothing did."

"What if the roles were reversed, and she told you it was the best sex she ever had—or that it was so bad she never wanted it again—but I was the one insisting nothing happened? Then how would this conversation go down?"

Mercy looked away. "I'd believe you."

"Why?"

"Susan's not much of the sleeping around type."

"She stuck her tongue down my throat and begged me to take her virginity." His voice rose, and he swallowed to bring his frustration under control. "Your sister isn't clueless." But suddenly, he understood Susan's argument on Friday night so much better. Mercy had gone out into the world, to live, but she was another voice keeping Susan from doing the same. And so was he. Fuck. Did that make him a hypocrite or a good guy? He didn't know anymore.

"Why did you want me to think you slept with her?" Mercy asked.

That was the billion-dollar question. "I was exhausted. Strung out. Not like that," he added when she raised her brows. "I figured you could put some distance between us." And that was what it came down to. He didn't know how many more times he could tell Susan *no*. The desire to turn her down wasn't there. But he'd do it for Mercy. *Would I really?*

"How's that working out for you?" Mercy's expression was sympathetic rather than judgmental.

"You're here instead of her. What do you think?"

She sighed. "I'm not trying to be overbearing or control her life. She's an adult, as you've so aptly pointed out. She can make up her own mind. But if she's a novelty to you... I don't want to see her get hurt."

"You got hurt." He didn't know why he was arguing. She'd made her point. He agreed. Except he didn't. He agreed with Susan, and not only for his own selfish reasons.

"I did. And it sucked so hard."

"But you lived. And you learned. And you grew. And you're here to debate with me now. I realize some things hurt more than others. I don't plan on being on that list. If you're giving me this kind of grief, what have you said to your dad?" *Whoa. Where did that come from?*

Her wide eyes said she wondered the same thing. "Nothing? Off topic much?"

"Not if we're talking about things that have the potential to wreck Susan's day. She hasn't told you." He should have known she was keeping potential roadblocks to her future plans to herself.

"Told me what? She asked me a couple of questions about why I left, because you were running your mouth."

"Because he's going to kick her out if she pursues dancing."

Mercy's jaw dropped. "I— No. He's learned."

"You'd know better than me. Do you believe it?"

"God *damn* it." She clenched her hand into a fist.

He was tired of arguing. "I meant it, when I said I'm not interested in corrupting her. She's there on her own, but that's a different story. I don't want to see her hurt, and if this was a shitstorm for you when he kicked you out, how's it going to be for her?"

"I'll take care of things with Dad if it comes to that. Make sure she's got a place to go. And I know everyone gets hurt, but some can be avoided, and that would be nice too."

"And… you're talking about me again."

Mercy stood, her gaze never leaving his. "What was it you told me seven years ago? Monogamy is fine for romantics and sheep, but you're never tying yourself to only one person?"

That was it exactly. Word for word, as far as he remembered. And she'd thrown back in his face the one reason he knew Susan deserved someone other than him.

"That's what I thought. You and me? We're good. But not if you break Susan's heart."

The conversation wilted to nothing, and a moment later Mercy left.

He let the conversation rent space in his skull, as it argued both perspectives, and he dove back into work. Minutes ticked away into hours, and he found the brain power to accomplish a few tasks. When the phone on his desk rang, he stared at it in confusion. Wrong number? He didn't know why anyone would call him here, rather than on his phone. "Hello?"

"Hey, Mister Andrew." It was Susan.

Despite his internal prompting to remain distant, hearing her drew a grin. "Hey, yourself."

"Did I offend you the other day?" Her cheerful tone cheered him across the lines.

"Not at all. It's that…" He didn't want to rehash the conversation he had with Mercy. Whatever the outcome, he'd lose. "It's complicated."

"It always is, with you. Promise to tell me the story next time I see you?"

This was where he needed to say, *That's done and over. You had your lessons. There's no reason for us to see each other again.* "Maybe not *next* time, but I promise." Like that, days of agonizing and self-abuse evaporated.

"I'm holding you to it. I only have a few minutes, but I had to call and thank you, and ask how things went with Lucas."

"Not well." The answer slipped out before he could consider it. "He told me he was happier believing the lie."

"I'm sorry." Sympathy hung heavy in the simple statement.

He wasn't used to this. Of course, any kind, socially-trained person was going to offer their condolences, but she sounded sincere. The way she always did.

He didn't need to be distracted by how good a person Susan was. He also wasn't interested in talking about the failed attempt to connect with his son. She'd said she called to thank him. "Thank me for what?"

"I thought a lot about what you said Friday night. About passion and pursuing what matters. I made a bunch of phone calls, and I've got an appointment lined up. I may be teaching dance at a studio down in the valley soon."

His smile grew, and an unfamiliar bubble of warmth spread through him. "That's fantastic." What he wanted to say next was *best of luck*. What came out instead was, "We should celebrate."

"It's a little premature for that." She laughed.

Fuck, he loved that sound. "This is a big deal, because it leads to more. I'm buying you lunch. Where can I meet you?" So much for keeping his distance. Though right now, that was the last thing he wanted to do.

"I can't do lunch. My interview is in Salt Lake, and I won't be back until this afternoon."

"Dinner then. Pick you up at home at six?"

"I can't wait."

How did such a simple conversation make his day? He didn't care to analyze it too far. The fact that it *did* was good enough for him.

Susan whirled through the kitchen, pivoted, then leaped the distance to the cupboard for a glass.

She'd fretted all weekend—far more than seemed reasonable—over whether or not to call Andrew. She was wounded he'd more or less turned her in to Mercy, but it meant she wasn't stranded. Whatever dragged him away from the hotel so early, he still looked out for Susan.

She decided this morning she couldn't be upset with Andrew unless she had a reason for his leaving. She wasn't going to make another mistake, like throwing herself at him, but asking what was up and making polite conversation was okay. When he invited her to dinner, the giddy little girl inside resurfaced, and she forgot about getting answers.

The interview this afternoon went wonderfully. She observed a class, hit it off with the studio director, and was going back later in the week, to help teach a beginner group.

Dad was working late, so she didn't have to answer any questions about her day. She had another interview tomorrow. She wasn't too proud to admit she had a charmed life.

Someone rang the bell, and she skip-twirled to answer. She stumbled when she found Andrew on the other side of the door. "You're early," she said.

"I finished work, and this was the most important thing on my calendar, so I put off everything else." And he had her flustered again. With a single statement. It had a little to do with the way the damp tips of his hair curled against his neck and the faintest hint of body wash that drifted from him.

She tugged him into the house. "Let me grab my purse, and we can go."

"I'm not the only one who's early." He followed her.

Her bag sat on the bar separating the dining room from the kitchen, her phone next to it. She swiped the screen out of habit, and saw she had a new message from Ballet West Institute. Her heart dropped into her stomach, and she hesitated with her thumb over the *Listen* prompt.

"Who's it from?" he asked.

"One of the studios I called over the weekend. It'll wait." She resisted the temptation, despite the pleading in her head to see what they wanted. *To tell me* no. She didn't know that.

"We have time. It'll kill you if you don't hear it now." He settled onto one of the stools next to the counter. "Besides, if you ignore it, you defeat the purpose of tonight."

"I do?"

"If we're celebrating that you're doing this, you have to actually do it."

She didn't want to argue with that, and was pulling up the message the moment the words were out of his mouth.

"Susan, this is Grace, with Ballet West. I saw you reached out to our Park City academy, to discuss a teaching

position. I definitely want to talk. I'm only here until six tonight, or you can call me in the morning."

Susan didn't know if she wanted to scream in excitement or cower from anxiety. She should probably get more information before she chose. The clock on her screen read five fifty-seven. She redialed the last incoming call, her pulse hammering in her ears with each ring.

"This is Grace."

"This is Susan Rice, returning your call." *Stay cool. Stay calm. Resist the urge to react, because nothing has happened yet.*

"Thank you for getting back to me. I heard you're looking for an instructor position."

Susan forced herself to breath, to keep the tremors from her voice. "That's right."

"I'm so glad you reached out. We've got a girl leaving on her Mormon mission next month. I haven't opened the slot yet, but I'd love sit down with you and discuss it." Grace laughed. "That's a formality. I already know you're talented, so as long as you're good with the students, I want you on staff."

Susan swallowed her squeal. "That sounds fantastic. When can we get together?"

They discussed details. Time. Place. If Susan had any salary requirements. The moment they disconnected, she dropped her phone and let out the happy cheer she'd been holding back.

"Good news?" Andrew looked amused.

"I guess so. Yes. I mean, not super amazing lead-in-the-Nutcracker huge. Or one of the fairies. But she wants me to teach. And it's a prestigious school. And"—she threw her arms around his neck, needing an outlet for the energy coursing through her—"thank you."

He squeezed her tight. "You don't have the job yet, and you did the hard work."

"But like you said this morning, it's a next step. It's progress." She pulled back, voice hitching when she caught his gaze—dark, intense, and she swore, trying to peer into her soul.

"I said that?" His tone dropped an octave. He dragged his fingers from her cheek to the back of her head, and caught her hair in a tight grip, never looking away from her. "Fuck. I'm smart."

"Brilliant." She forced out the word.

When he crashed his mouth down on hers, her pulse threatened to tear from her veins. This wasn't like the last two times. The way he smashed against her lips, nibbling then claiming... It was hungry. Unrestrained. Terrifying. And—holy hell—she wanted more.

EIGHTEEN

Andrew pulled Susan between his legs, not easing up on the kiss. She molded her body to his, every inch of contact searing across his skin and burrowing deeper. He was fucking tired of fighting this attraction. He tugged her head back, to suck a line down to her collarbone. The way she shifted against him pressed buttons he didn't know he had. How was this possible? This intoxicating woman made him feel like a teenage boy with out of control hormones. The only clear thought he had was about fucking her.

He traced his tongue up the side of her neck. She even *tasted* like cookies. When he pushed up the bottom of her shirt, she dug her fingers into his arms with a whimper. His dick begged to be free, straining against his jeans to be closer to the heat taunting him. He grabbed sufficient rational thought to look her in the eyes. Clear. Blue. Captivating…

"This doesn't change anything between us. It doesn't make us a couple. Nothing like that," he said.

"I know." She licked her lips, and he wanted to kiss away the shine. Suck on that almost-pout until she couldn't think.

"Is someone going to walk in on us?"

"Do you care?"

Right now? He only cared about one thing. "I really don't. You don't need the grief, though."

"No one will be home until late. No one's walking in on us. Don't you dare try to talk us out of this again. Please?"

This was all he needed to hear. Except maybe a little more of her begging. He dove back in without hesitation, scraping his teeth along her shoulder, then sucking on her neck. He glided a hand under her top and slid his palm up her bare stomach to her breast, to trail his thumb over her bra and the swollen nipple underneath. Each tiny gasp she let out stole more of his reason. He pinched the hard nub through fabric, and she squirmed against him.

It had been ages since an action as simple as making out felt so intense. High school? Had it ever? He couldn't remember.

She worked a hand between them and moved it below his waist. When she cupped his cock through his jeans—a tentative, teasing touch—he jerked against her. If she decided to grip or stroke, he'd probably come right now.

Outside, evening traffic droned by. Garage doors opened. Neighbors chattered. None of it mattered but what was going on in here. He pushed her clothes out of the way and nibbled through the lace of her bra. Her light giggle spurred him on.

One of the neighbors sounded familiar, and damn their doors were loud.

"What the *hell* is going on here?" An older male voice shattered the mood.

Apparently this was about to be a lot more like high school than Andrew wanted. Susan back-pedaled several feet, yanking her top down as she moved. Her cheeks flushed from pink to glowing fuchsia in a blink. "Daddy. I thought you had work to do."

"I needed some paperwork he left at home." And that was Mercy.

Jesus-fucking-Christ. Andrew summoned a neutral expression, hopped to his feet, and turned to face the new arrivals. They stood in the doorway between the kitchen and the garage. They stood in the doorway between the kitchen and the garage— Dean Rice watching him with a touch of murder in his gaze, and Mercy frowning, arms crossed.

"We were talking. *Celebrating.*" Susan's words ran together.

Mercy raised her brows. "Good word."

"Get the hell out of my house"—Dean took a step forward, speaking between clenched teeth—"or I'll have the police here so fast—"

"Dad, stop for a minute." Mercy's soft tone cut through the rage.

It was one of the rare moments in Andrew's life he was at a loss for what to say. He wanted to swivel his head back and forth, watching the tennis match.

Dean didn't look at Mercy when he replied to her. "I don't have to like who you do business with, but you have no right to bring this filth into my home. Into *our* lives."

"Hey now." Andrew bit his tongue to keep *I took a shower before I came over* from slipping out.

Mercy blocked her father's path. "Stop. We're all adults here."

Susan touched Andrew's arm, and a jolt raced through leather and fabric and his skin. "Go. Please?" Her voice was soft.

He'd been wrong—he had no interest in hearing her beg again. Not like this. The simple request beat him down harder than any insult. He didn't have a right to be hurt, but it dug deep that her first instinct was to push him away. "Yeah. That's a good idea." He didn't look at anyone, but turned and walked out the front door. What did he expect? He made it clear to Susan from the start—and as recently as a few minutes ago—they were friends at best. Acknowledging this didn't ease the ache in his heart.

He wasn't sinking into this hole. He'd asked for an impetus to keep them apart. This was it. Work waited, and that meant a lot of pussy to look at that wasn't mired in things like family and daddy issues —he'd review those sites a different day.

DAD FACED SUSAN, face red and scowl etched in stone. "Explain."

She didn't know what to say first. "I was happy. I got good news. He was here…" Crap, that came out wrong. Susan's brain was so twisted in on itself, she couldn't think. "I mean, I got a new job. Maybe. This wasn't what it looked like."

"What kind of job?" Despite the lilt to her dad's words, anger radiated from him.

Mercy stood to the side, drumming her fingers against her leg and looking like she was struggling to keep her mouth shut.

"Teaching." Uncertainty kept the entire truth from coming out. Like the *where.* "It's not for sure yet, but I'm pretty close."

"You haven't graduated. Where are you going to teach without a degree?" he said.

Say the words. Tell him the truth. "It's a private, charter kind of thing."

185

"Not a reputable one if you don't need a degree. What are they called?"

She looked at Mercy, as if she might find answers there. Mercy's face was pinched with sympathy, but her only response was a shrug.

"Ballet West." Susan forced out the words. "Their academy in Park City is about to open a position for instructor, and they want to talk to me."

"I see." His voice took on a level of calm she only heard when he was furious. "Get out."

"What?" She was told this could happen, by two different people. That didn't make the words easier to hear or believe. She misunderstood. He didn't mean for good.

"You were warned. Leave the phone and the car keys. I paid for your clothes as well, but I don't know what I'd do with them."

Susan didn't understand. "But... It's a stepping stone. A reputable job that I love."

"It's prancing around like a fool, in practically nothing, *and* teaching other little girls it's okay to do the same. Whoring yourself out, the same way your sister did."

"*Whoa,*" Mercy said.

But Susan couldn't let that go unchecked. "Melissa is not a whore. Neither am I. We're not freaking—I don't know—*Quakers* or whatever. Dance isn't against your religion. This is a celebration of movement."

"It's not the dance I have a problem with; it's the way you do it. The ideas you associate with it. The rebellion that led you to go against my request in the first place. Do you want to be a stripper at a sleazy club in Wendover?"

Susan struggled to believe this conversation was real, but that didn't mean she'd flinch away from it. "They're nice girls."

"Definitely sweeter than some of those from church," Mercy added.

"This isn't a discussion. You won't live under my roof if this is the path you're going to take. Get. Out."

"*Stop.*" Mercy's voice grew in volume. "She's not doing anything wrong. She's your fucking daughter. You've only got the one left."

Her meaning spread through Susan on a cloud of realization. This was breaking the tentative relationship Mercy finally had with him.

"She's done everything wrong." Dad's words hollowed Susan out, leaving a painful vacuum behind. "Defied my requests. Mocked my beliefs." He looked at Mercy. "What did you do? Sell her to your *business partner*, the moment I let you back in the house?"

Mercy looked at Susan. "Let's go."

He stepped in her path. "You wanted to have this conversation. Let's have it. You threw a tantrum ten years ago and stormed out. Don't discard Susan's life too."

"Excuse me? Wanting to think for myself is *throwing a tantrum?*"

"Being an unreasonable child is. I wasn't going to say anything when that friend of yours showed up at your wedding; your associates are your business. Speaking of business—Ian's clients are none of mine, until it impacts my revenue."

Susan didn't know what to say. The cold words chewed at her world.

Mercy wasn't held back by the same doubt. Or any doubt, apparently. She stood toe to toe with Dad, anger flashing in her eyes. "Smut Central is *my* client. Not Ian's. Remember the *R* in R&T? It stands for Rowe. Not Thompson. *Not* Rice. Andrew's also a good friend. I trust him with my life, which is a hell of a lot more than I can say for you."

Why wasn't Susan saying these things? The words wouldn't come.

"That's your mistake. One of thousands, I'm sure." Dad—Susan didn't want to call him such a personal name right now. *Mr. Rice?*—didn't back down.

Mercy's smile looked twisted and dark. "Let's talk about mistakes. We'll ignore the one you're making tonight. Why did it take so long for you to reach out to me? If you were sorry about the way things transpired between us, why did you wait until I was here for Liz's wedding, to extend the olive branch? I begged you to talk to me, more than once. Liz has known how to find me since I left. There's never been any mystery about my location. And then, the first time you saw me in ten years, you insulted me. Days later, you wanted to make up?"

"You're right; reaching out to you again was a mistake. You were dating someone respectable—finally. The only reason I asked Ian to put me in touch with you was because Susan wanted it, and I hoped he'd tempered you, so you wouldn't exacerbate her condition."

"My *condition*?" Susan didn't know what else to do.

Mercy shook her head. "That's nice. Real loving and caring. So this was never about making amends."

"I'm proud of what you've done"—his words might have carried more weight at any other time—"but not the way you got here. I hoped with Ian, you'd grown up. Your sister is making the same mistakes you did, and my hope was you could teach her not to be stupid."

Numbness set in. Susan felt a scab forming inside—a reaction to too much of an onslaught at once. "Do you hear yourself?" she asked. "You forced your own daughter out of the house, and now you're going to do it again? Because we don't conform to your standards?"

He looked at her. Or through her. This was worse. "Instead of helping you mature, she introduced you to that gigolo pimp she lets follow her around like a lost puppy. At the very least, Melissa has a career. You won't have that."

"Don't you—"

"*Shut up.*" Susan cut Mercy off. She did what he'd requested, and left her phone and car keys on the bar. She didn't trust herself to say anything else. She walked past her sister and the man next to her, out the door and through the garage, and stopped next to Mercy's car. Cold air permeated her lungs. She wasn't wearing a coat. Not that she cared.

"Hey." Mercy settled a hand on her shoulder. "I'm sorry. I didn't mean... I never wanted this to happen to you."

Susan used the icy night to chill her words, but she couldn't face her sister. "I know. It was my decision, and I made it, and I'm sticking to it."

"Are you okay?"

"No." Susan couldn't hold back the tears stinging her eyelids and burning down her face.

Mercy hugged her from behind. "I'm so sorry."

NINETEEN

Susan overheard Mercy and Ian talking in hushed tones in the study, when she drew close. *Hushed* was a good word for the mood of the house tonight.

"I never thought it would come down to this." Ian sounded frustrated.

Mercy was pacing. "I should have guessed, but after all the *I'm sorry's*... it's a bit of a blindside."

That was one way to put it. The numbness in Susan had given way to a persistent ache. Her father didn't want her. Twenty-one was probably too old to cry about things like *Daddy kicked me out*, but his reasons—those harsh words—hurt so much.

"If you want us to cancel their contract, we will," Ian said. "I've questioned doing business with them for a long time, and this is one of those things I won't tolerate."

Mercy shook her head. "That's business. You can't confuse it with personal matters."

"It's both. They're family businesses, and sometimes those lines have to blur."

"I don't know." Mercy spat out the words. "I want to say it was an emotional moment, and things will be better once everyone calms down, but I'm done with him."

Susan moved away from the doorway and into the shadows before they could see her. She pressed her back to the wall and slid to the floor. This sucked.

"Come here." Ian's voice filtered into the hallway. "I kind of hate you found *him* to help pick up the pieces last time this happened, and I wasn't there to stop you from running so far away."

Mercy's chuckle mingled with a sigh. "He's got a name. There's no way you're jealous of Andrew."

"Nope. I wouldn't trade you for all the pictures of naked women in the world. But my point is I'm here this time, whatever you or Susan need."

"You're such a sweet-talker." Some of the stress vanished from Mercy's voice.

A spark of jealousy flashed through Susan, and she made her way to her room before she had to hear more. It must be nice to have that kind of love.

Susan considered reaching out to her brothers or other sister. She nixed the idea moments after it surfaced, based on the cruelty they directed at

Mercy when she left home. Only one of them forgave her when she came back into their lives, and it was a more tentative truce than Mercy shared with Dad.

Night blurred into morning, punctuated by restless sleep and struggling to process how she'd been tossed out of her childhood home as if she were a stray cat, rather than her father's daughter.

Susan poured a glass of juice, trying to figure out what to do with her sudden free time now that she was out of a job. Call the various dance studios back. Make sure they had the house number here, to get a hold of her. Fortunately, her contacts were associated with her email, so she didn't lose everything when she surrendered her phone.

"Hey." Mercy wandered into the kitchen, Ian behind her. They were dressed for work. "How are you holding up?"

Susan gave her a thin smile, not able to put her feelings into words. She handed Ian the juice when he reached for it.

"After work, I'll take you to pick up a new phone and some stuff to wear, until we can get your clothes back. Feel free to raid my closet," Mercy said.

"Thanks. But I'll pay you back, I promise." Susan hated that she couldn't fend for herself. No job. No money. No car. She was lucky she had *some* family.

Ian finished his drink, then rinsed the glass and

set it in the sink. He tossed Mercy her car keys, from the pegs near the garage door. "Don't worry about it," he said. "Save your money—whatever you've got from your last paycheck. Stretch it out while you can."

"I didn't get a paycheck. Like *ever*. I was an intern." She realized now how stupid the words sounded.

"You *what*?" Mercy's voice rose.

Anger flashed across Ian's face. "You weren't an intern, because you're a Fine Arts major, not a Business student. He never paid you?"

Susan shook her head, staring at the tiles on the counter.

"That answers that question," Ian said. "I'll talk to Legal today. See how quickly we can terminate their contract."

Susan hated the idea, though she liked the sentiment. "No. You can't hurt your company just because of me."

Mercy nudged Susan's fingers, to draw her attention. "We would. *Just* because of you. But the only reason we haven't booted Rice Real Estate before now is because they're an old client. They don't do TV, or internet. Doesn't matter that Dad is worth billions; he's not spending it on advertising. His company is such a teensy drop of our revenue, it won't matter." She looked amused saying those words. "Besides, if we found out they were doing this to anyone, we'd dump them. It happens faster because there's bad blood."

"Liz mentioned a few days ago she's got an opening for an assistant, if you're interested," Ian offered.

Getting a different job—the thing that cost her all of this. "I have interviews lined up from before. But if they don't pan out…" Then again, teaching dance a couple nights a week wouldn't pay the bills. It was winter break, so she had time to formulate a plan before she went back to school. Was she going back to school? Not if she couldn't pay for it. Could she do anything for herself? She slouched back against the counter in frustration.

"How are you holding up?" Mercy asked again.

"I don't know. How long did it take before you could shake it off?"

"You don't want that answer."

"I'll ask Andrew." Crap. She owed him an apology too. Mercy stood up for him; Susan whimpered while Dad tore everyone apart.

Ian arched a single brow. "Mercy, do you want me to tell KaleidoMation you'll be late or that you can't make it today?" He sounded concerned, not irritated.

Mercy looked at Susan.

"Go," Susan said. "I'll be fine."

"It took a long time, but it helped that I didn't

have to do it alone. Neither do you." Mercy gave her a quick hug. "See you tonight."

Susan's mind tripped over everything, replaying the fight with Dad until she might scream. She couldn't make it stop, though. Not through the shower. Or getting dressed—she was fortunate she had some clothes here. Or eating something for breakfast that said it was oatmeal, but might as well have been sawdust for as much as she tasted it.

It took a couple of hours to find the motivation, but eventually she forced herself to sit down in front of a computer in the study and log into her accounts. The first few calls she made, she grinned through gritted teeth to sound pleasant, but the acting sank in, helping to mask some of the chaos raging inside.

ANDREW WAS BOTHERED by how hard it was to get Susan out of his head. But it was because he was worried. Now that some of the blood had flowed back to his brain and he was thinking more clearly, he saw she made a reasonable request last night. After he grabbed two minutes of Mercy's time in the office, to get a brief what happened after he left, he wished he'd stuck around and decked Dean Rice.

What Mercy didn't say, the unspoken details reflected in her eyes, worried him as much as the news Dean had made good on his threat to evict Susan. Thoughts of her distracted Andrew the rest of the morning—story of his life since he got here. It would be nice to get back home, where he actually got work done.

The thought pinged in his chest, and he shook it aside before knocking on Mercy's front door.

The Susan who answered looked different from what he was used to. Her hair drooped, rather than the spikes she preferred, and her smile didn't reach her eyes. "Hey." She leaned against the door, rather than inviting him in. "What's up?" Her voice was flat. That was worse than her asking him to leave.

"Mercy told me what happened. Sort of. I have a little more of a flexible schedule than most people, so I wanted to check on you."

Her fake smile vanished. "So she asked you to drop by."

"No. Mercy is a good excuse, but this has always been about you." Until he said the words, he didn't realize how true they were.

The corners of her eyes tugged up. "I figured, after everything, you'd hate me."

"I was a little pissed off. Wounded. Really fucking horny. One makes the other two worse, but I've had time to cool down."

"Then you're here for sex stuff?"

Despite being broken hearted and bummed out, she was still her. Andrew liked that. "I'm not ruling it out, but I'm here for you. Besides, I stole your brother-in-law's credit card. Figured we'd go shopping."

"No, you didn't." This smile came with a tiny laugh, making the joke worth it.

"Well, no. But think of all the potential there. We could have an afternoon mall-montage, like in Clueless."

Her smile grew. "You mean that old movie about the rich girl who realizes life is about more than money and popularity contests? The scene where she's hitting on the sexy guy until she realizes he's into guys more than her? Oh heck. My life is a stupid nineties teen movie."

"Old. *Pfft.* Lunch?" He ignored the comment about the sexy guy on purpose. Correcting her—saying she was without a question the only person he'd fantasized about in over a week—would be a bad idea. Mercy had one thing right. He wasn't relationship material.

She opened the door wider. "I have to make a couple more calls. I'm updating my contact information with dance studios. Do you have time to wait?"

"I've got the entire afternoon." He joined her inside. It was good she hadn't given up on her dancing. He followed her into the study.

She dropped into a chair. "Ten minutes, tops."

"Take your time. Really." He pulled up a seat,

flipped it back toward her to straddle it, and rested his chin on the back. "I'll sit here and watch. Nothing creepy." This time he got a real laugh from her. Perfect.

"Not creepy at all." She turned her attention back to the computer and the cordless phone next to it.

Despite the joke, Andrew didn't know what to do with his time. He tripped his gaze around the room, glancing over a wall of leather-bound books he suspected no one had read in years, an antique-looking globe that was probably only a couple decades old, and a crystal brandy set. *Cliché.*

He turned back to Susan. Definitely the best view in the room. The way she chewed on her lip when she was focused—the twitches that flew across her face as she poured herself into the conversation… She had to be hurting inside, but it vanished when she dove into a call and started chatting.

She looked up as she disconnected, and pink spread across her cheeks. "I didn't think you were actually going to stare."

"The scenery is good." He closed his eyes. "Better?"

"Sure. Why not," she said. When he looked again, she was back on the phone, but glancing at him every few seconds. "Hi, this is Susan Rice. We talked last night." Her tone went from playful to chipper and professional in a breath. "I'm sorry to bother you during your work day, but I wanted to get you my updated contact information and make sure the timing was still good for our appointment." Her expression melted. "I see. May I ask why?" A scowl moved in, twisting her mouth and painting lines across her forehead. "No. I understand... Of course not. This is what you have to do. Thank you anyway for your time."

Susan pressed a button on the phone, then set it on the desk. She took a deep breath. "God-damn-asshole-fucking-son-of-a-bitch-bastard. *Fuck.*" She dropped her head into her hands.

"That good, huh?" He didn't have anything better. Not after an outburst like that.

Her shoulders shook, and she rubbed her face several times before looking up. "Grace got a call from my father's charitable foundation this morning. They're reevaluating how to best spend their donations next year, and... My freaking dad."

Andrew knew how the thought ended. Whatever conversation transpired between this Grace and Dean Rice this morning made it clear that hiring Susan would impact those donations as they related to Ballet West. He had much stronger language for the situation than she'd used, and he regretted more that he didn't stick around long enough last night to throw that punch.

TWENTY

IT DIDN'T MATTER HOW DEEP INTO THE RECESSES OF his brain Andrew reached, he couldn't find a witty story or clever joke or sexy anecdote for the situation. Susan insisted she wanted to join him for lunch, that it was miles better than being stuck in the house, alone with her thoughts.

Now she sat across from him, picking at her pasta, and not eating anything.

"It's true, there are other options." She stabbed a noodle. "I haven't exhausted my Round One." She speared a piece of chicken. "But this chance was so good, and—" She dropped her fork, and it clattered to the plate. "Why is he doing this? What did I do wrong?"

Andrew didn't want to filter his thoughts. It wasn't a priority for him under normal circumstances, and this was anything but. However, he had a feeling *he's a vile old man who hates anyone who isn't like him* was the wrong answer. He didn't know how to approach this. "You didn't do anything wrong. If he can't accept that, it's not your fault."

That drew a flash of a smile that faded in an instant.

Andrew had the waiter box up the rest of Susan's lunch, paid, then pulled her to her feet. "Come on," he said.

"I don't think I'm up for a mall montage, if that's where we're going." She didn't withdraw her hand from his as they walked toward the parking lot.

He intertwined their fingers. "It's not. I'm not taking you shopping unless I get to help you try on clothes."

"You have to wait until tomorrow for that." She peeked up at him through her lashes.

"Why tomorrow?"

"I figure I'll be all cured and happy again by then. Sleep and chocolate fix everything, don't they?"

"I think that's exactly how it works." He wouldn't call her on the false cheer. A genuine hope lingered underneath, and that was a nice change. "I'm going to kidnap you for the rest of the afternoon and evening. Unless you have objections."

"I get a say in my own kidnapping? Seems dangerous. No objections."

He drove along one of the back roads, twisting and winding toward the summit—a location he discovered a couple trips ago that always seemed to be deserted. She probably saw views like it all the time, growing up, but he thought it was stunning, and it would do her some good to get away from everything for a few hours. They didn't say much on the half-hour drive. Each time he glanced at her, she was staring out the window, the glass reflecting her sad expression.

He parked a few feet from the main road, and took her hand when she hopped from the SUV. Snow-covered trees stretched out behind them, and a guardrail separated the road from a several-hundred-foot drop.

Susan made her way to the edge and looked down. A soft gasp floated from her. "It's gorgeous. I didn't know a spot like this existed." She spun, to see more of the landscape, never untangling her fingers from his. Her awe was contagious. Nearly tangible.

"You've never been up here?" he asked.

"No. I love it." A sharp gust of wind tore through the afternoon, and she shivered.

He wrapped his arms around her and pulled her back into his chest, not realizing what he'd done until he held her close. Didn't matter. He wasn't interested in letting go. Especially when she leaned more weight into him.

"I was driving. I stumbled on it." He rested his

chin on her shoulder and kept his voice low. His phone rang, shattering the mood. It was Kandace. "I should get this."

"IT'S FINE." Susan took a few steps back. Some of the lines had vanished from around her eyes and mouth, and her voice was lighter than earlier.

"Hey, sis."

"Oh God. I'm so glad you're there. Lucas is missing."

The bottom dropped from Andrew's world. It wasn't just the words, but her panicked tone. "Missing, how? When?"

"He stayed at a friend's last night after therapy. I got a text from him, saying he was there, and another this morning, checking in. But the school called, and he never showed up. His friend's mother says he was gone before she woke up. His friend said he left in the middle of the night, crying, but he didn't want to wake up his parents, because he was scared they'd be mad, so he didn't tell them until after school."

Jesus. Andrew rested against the SUV, thoughts spinning out of control. "It's a fluke. He's somewhere safe, and his phone is dead. What did the cops say?" He didn't have to ask if she called them.

"They're asking questions. Have a current picture. He's only ten. They just left to start looking, and I'm going to gather everyone in the neighborhood. I hope you're right and he's someplace I haven't thought of."

"I'll be there in an hour. Forty-five minutes if I punch it. Call me if anything changes." He was going to be sick. It didn't matter how many reassurances he sent through his head, none stuck. He disconnected and looked up, to see Susan standing next to him.

"I'm going with you," she said.

He didn't have the mental power to argue or process how much she overheard. "Fine. Good. Get in the car."

He gripped the wheel until his knuckles ached, as they headed down the canyon. The roads weren't icy—he had that to be grateful for—and it was only three, so traffic was light. What the hell had happened? Silence hummed in his ears, and a couple of times he swore he heard the opening notes of his ringtone. But it was his imagination.

It took what little self-control Andrew had left, not to press the gas pedal through the floor of the vehicle. Lucas had been gone for more than twelve hours. It was barely above freezing outside. If he wasn't at a neighbor's house or the school, and none of the local businesses had seen him, where was he?

Susan settled her hand on his leg, near the knee. The gentle touch sent an odd ribbon of calm to wrap around his tension, but didn't stop it. "He's okay. You'll find him," she said.

"Yeah. Of course." He didn't believe his reply. There was no way *she* bought it.

A million horrific scenarios tortured him, and he tried to shove them back with ideas about where Lucas might be. He'd have a better idea if he spent more time here. *Fuck*. Why hadn't he spent more time with the boy? Where could Lucas be? Did he wander off and hide, or had he been snatched?

They arrived at Kandace's, and the closest available parking spot was several houses down. Police cars lined the street, and neighbors and cops milled in and out of the house.

He wove through all of them, and the moment Kandace saw him, she gave him a huge hug. Lines marred her face. "I don't know what to do," she said.

"We'll find him." He rubbed her back before letting her go. "Where do you need us?"

She raked her fingers through her hair. "I don't know. People are roaming the streets."

He could join them and be another useless body. It wasn't as though he thought Lucas would answer to him if the boy was ignoring everyone else.

"Ma'am." One of the officers interrupted. "We just got off the phone with the district. The bus driver says he was on the bus this morning. You're sure no one at the school saw him?"

She shook her head. "That's what they told me when they called."

When I was little, and the sisters would rap my knuckles for things that weren't my fault, like holes worn in the elbows of my uniform, I'd hide out there. The words slammed into Andrew's head like a bullet, knocking aside everything else. He'd told Lucas that years ago, when they were talking about the school Lucas would go to. *Please, Jesus, let it be this simple.*

He grabbed Kandace's arm. "I have an idea. I don't know if it will pan out, but I'm going to look. The old nursery on Fifth, near Twenty-First."

Kandace nodded. "Good luck."

Susan followed him back to the car. He tossed her his phone before he pulled onto the street. "In case you need to call Kandace. Code is 80085."

It couldn't be this simple, but he had to check. As he navigated city streets and cursed every red light, Susan gave his knee another squeeze. "Only you and about every five-year-old on the planet would think that was funny." Teasing mingled with her concerned tone.

Her comment drew a smile, despite his tension. She was talking about his passcode. "What can I say? I'm predictable." Moments later, he turned into the lot behind a convenience store. Calling it *paved* would be an overstatement. Dead weeds jabbed through the cracks in the asphalt. Like it was twenty years ago. He didn't wait to see if Susan followed.

He hopped from the SUV, and picked his way over broken concrete blocks and torn pieces of fence, to the abandoned building next door.

Since he was here last, they'd boarded up the windows and padlocked the back door. He pried at each piece of plywood, his fingertips sore by the time he got to the last one. None of them gave. The chain on the door was rusted, but held when he rattled it.

No way in. He sighed and leaned back against the building. So much for that idea. They needed to get back to Kandace, but if she hadn't called, she didn't have any news.

"Andrew?" Susan called from around the corner. He kicked away from the filthy brick and moved to find her. She was kneeling next to a pile of crumbled wall. It was tough to make out details in the shadows and fading light, but it looked like a hole. "Hand me your phone again." She held out her hand.

He switched on the flashlight and handed it over. She dropped to her stomach and shone the light around. With each passing second, he prayed a little harder, though he wasn't sure what for.

"I'll be right back." She was crawling through the opening before he could ask for more details.

"Be careful," he said.

Milliseconds passed, seeming to take centuries, before she yelled, "Get in here, *now.*"

"How?" The hole was too narrow for his shoulders, so that wasn't an option.

She didn't answer. A moment later, he heard her muffled voice. "Yes. I'm at an abandoned shop on Fifth east and about Twenty-Third south, behind the Exxon. I need an ambulance. Male. Unconscious. Ten. He's breathing, yes."

That spurred Andrew into action. He sprinted back to the SUV and tore the back apart until he found the spare tire. He grabbed the lug-nut wrench, grateful it had a crowbar wedge on the other side, and ran back to the shop. He'd pry off the plywood or break through it somehow. He didn't care. He had to get in there.

ANDREW SAT in a waiting room seat, knee bouncing and jaw clenched. Kandace paced a few feet away. He wanted to tell her to sit down, but he didn't have the mental capacity to form words. Susan hadn't left his side since they loaded Lucas into the ambulance, but she hadn't said anything either. He was grateful for both.

"Ms. Newton?" A man in scrubs and a hair cap headed for Kandace. He nodded toward a side door. "Do you want to join me in here, and we'll talk?"

She shook her head. "No. They need to hear this. What's going on?"

The doctor sat and patted the spot next to him. "We treated him based on what was found around him. The liquor and empty prescription bottle."

Like father, like son. Andrew kept the bitter thought to himself.

The doctor continued. "There's no way to know how long ago he took them, and it will take time to confirm that's all he's got in his system. He's on respiration and fluids. His vitals are steady, but he's not out of the woods yet. Once he wakes up, we'll be more confident with his diagnosis."

"Can I sit with him until then?" Kandace asked.

"Yes. But"—the doctor frowned—"you'll need to talk to the police, first. They're waiting."

This was too much for Andrew. "The boy is lying unconscious in a fucking hospital bed, and you want her to answer some piddly fucking questions?"

"Stop." Kandace shot him a warning look.

The doctor looked sympathetic. "I'm sorry, but it's the law. He's a minor, he's injured, this looks like a suicide attempt, and he got the pills and liquor from somewhere. You can see him and then speak with them in a nearby room. They've been patient waiting until we had answers, I'll ask them to give you ten more minutes so you can see your son."

Andrew wanted to protest. To rant and rave about how Kandace was an amazing parent who this was obviously destroying, and how dare they question that? But doing so would add to her stress. He had to bite his tongue until it ached.

The three followed the doctor through a series of doors, upstairs in the elevator, and through more doors, before he gestured to a room. As the doctor warned, two police officers waited in the hallway. They had the courtesy to step aside when Kandace rushed toward Lucas. Andrew followed.

Lucas lay in the middle of a too-big for him bed, wires running to monitors, a tube connected to a bag, and a mask with what Andrew assumed was a tube running down his throat. The boy looked smaller than normal. *Suicide attempt.* The doctor's words rang in is ears. *Pills and liquor.* He wanted to say Lucas wouldn't do that, but he hadn't spent enough time here, to know. Was it Andrew's revelation on Saturday that caused this, or was that a selfish thought?

He stared at the frail body, so many questions tormenting him. Why did this happen?

TWENTY-ONE

Susan touched Andrew's shoulder, and he pulled his gaze from Lucas to look at her, as if he'd forgotten the rest of the world. The conversation with the police didn't take long. They were involved in the search earlier and sympathetic to Kandace's plight.

Susan tugged the sleeve of Andrew's coat. "You're going to be here for a while. Might as well take this off," she said gently.

"Right. Thanks." He shrugged out of the jacket and let her take it.

He turned his attention back to the bed before she finished draping his jacket and hers over a chair. She repeated the gesture with Kandace, whose look was equally haunted.

In a way, it felt wrong to be here. As if she was intruding on too private a moment for an outsider.

At the same time, she didn't want to leave them alone. This was what it looked like when family cared. In a twisted way, she envied Lucas. Not his situation, but if it had been her, hurt or lost, would her father care beyond how it would damage his image in the community?

She shook aside the venom-filled and selfish thought, and dragged a chair in from another room. When the legs scraped against tile, screeching through the quiet, she cringed. Neither Andrew nor Kandace looked up. She positioned herself next to Andrew and intertwined her fingers with his.

He squeezed until their hands shook, and then relaxed his grip with a sigh. "I'm sorry."

"Don't be."

"Thank you for finding him." Andrew's voice was barely more than a whisper.

"You got us there. I helped finish the thought."

"Thank you anyway. I don't know what I'd do if…"

She traced her thumb over his. "I know, but that's not how it went down, so it's not worth dwelling on."

"You're pretty smart sometimes, Suzie-Q."

"What can I say? It's a gift."

Silence descended again, smothering until Susan had to remind herself nothing had changed in the air. That she could breathe fine.

Someone knocked lightly on the open hospital

door, and the three swiveled their heads toward the sound. A woman stood there with a boy about Lucas's age, whose eyes were red rimmed and puffy.

"Rose." Kandace's voice sounded like it filtered through sandpaper. She cleared her throat. "What's up?"

Rose nudged the boy forward. "I don't want to interrupt, but Noah needs to talk to you. He insisted. Go ahead, honey."

"It's my fault. I'm sorry." Noah started sobbing and shaking, until Susan worried he might rattle apart.

Rose knelt behind him and hugged him. "It's okay. They won't be mad."

Andrew's grip sent a tremor through Susan's arm. For several minutes, the loudest sound in the room was the boy's cries, mingling with his mother's wordless whisper.

Noah hiccupped and sniffled. He looked up again. "A few weeks ago, at school, Lucas kissed me. And I liked it." He searched the faces in the room, as if he were terrified that alone would get him in trouble. "So last night, I thought it was okay. And we were playing, and I kissed him back. And he got so mad, and told me he hated me and he hated himself and he wished he'd never been born. And that's when he left."

Andrew hissed, low and long. Susan didn't know if anyone else heard.

Kandace slid from her chair, to crouch next to Noah. She looked him in the eye. "Thank you for telling us," she said. "You're not in trouble. And this isn't your fault. Do you understand?"

He nodded. "Will Lucas be okay?"

Susan's gut clenched at the pause.

"Of course he will. He'll stay at your house again soon, if you want." Kandace gave him an awkward hug. She talked to Rose for a minute or two in hushed tones, then mother and son left.

"Conversion therapy won't be a big deal." Andrew's tone was snide. "It's his decision. He'll be fine."

The look Kandace shot him would have wilted any plant in its path. "That's helpful."

Andrew growled and stomped to his feet. "I need some air." He looked at Susan. "Keep me company?"

She nodded. The way he pulled her to stand, his arm around her waist, and the tender gestures felt natural. She waited until they made it down the hallway, to a waiting room with a window over-looking the parking garage, before speaking. "How are you doing?"

"I feel like shit." He turned his back to the glass and leaned against the wall underneath, before tugging her to face him. He trailed his gaze over her. "You're a mess."

She looked down. She was covered in dirt from

crawling into the abandoned building. Brushing it away didn't do her any good. "I guess so."

"I should get you a ride home." He didn't move.

"I'd rather stay here. Make sure Lucas is all right. That you are. Unless you want me to go."

"I really don't."

"Then I'm staying."

He kicked from the wall and paced to another window at the far end of the room, and she stayed by his side. "I didn't meet him for the first time until he was three." Andrew stared out at the night. "Before then, I sent any spare cash back home to help Kandace. Buying a plane ticket home felt self-ish, when I barely had any money as it was. When I saw him... There was no doubt he had my genes. Same gorgeous hair and swoon-worthy eyes."

She leaned her arm into his. At least Andrew was himself, under the worry and grief. "I see that in him," she said. "He'll be a different kind of sweet-talker than you are, though."

"As in, he'll actually sweet-talk?"

"Sounds right."

Andrew let out a forced chuckle. "It was hard for me to leave after that trip. Lucas was so happy with Kandace, though. And she obviously loved him. I was getting the business off the ground, and I'd never had that kind of money before. It was easy to convince myself I needed to get back out into the world, in order to keep things growing. I went back about six months later. It was harder to leave that time. After that, I got really good at making excuses for why I couldn't come visit. I was terrified my being here would disrupt the life Kandace built for them."

She'd heard this tone from him before. Seen the look in his eyes. Recognized the way he sounded like he was falling into the past. It was the same as when he told her the story about Belgium. Like then, pain on his behalf gnawed at her joints and echoed through her veins. Nothing she said would alleviate whatever tormented him.

He gripped the ledge until his knuckles turned red, then white. "When Mercy moved back here earlier this year, and I started flying out for meetings, I spent more and more time with Lucas and Kandace. I decided I didn't want to be cut out of their lives anymore. Now… I wonder if I was being selfish again."

"You didn't cause this any more than that boy did."

"I know. Or I tell myself I do. The mind plays funny tricks during times like this."

She loosened his grip, to slide her hand under his, palm up. "You're here now, and so is he. You've got time."

"Yeah. We should get back."

She nodded, though he didn't see. They settled back into Lucas's room and waited. She didn't know how much time passed. An hour? Two? A ring filled the room. Andrew and Kandace didn't look up. Susan fumbled in her jacket pocket, realizing she hadn't returned Andrew's phone. Mercy's name was on the screen. Susan squeezed Andrew's shoulder, then headed into the hallway.

"Hey." She kept her voice low.

"Thank God you're all right. I know I shouldn't worry—you're an adult and all—but you don't have a phone or a car and you didn't come home. You *are* okay, aren't you?"

The concern soothed Susan more than she expected. "*I* am, but I don't know when I'll be back."

"What's going on?"

A spark of warmth spread through Susan at the questions. She gave Mercy a brief run-down of the last several hours.

"I don't know what to say. How are Andrew and Kandace holding up?" Mercy asked.

"A lot of staring and worrying. About what you'd expect."

"Call me if you have news but don't make me a priority. And, hey."

"Hmm…?" Susan said.

"Someone should be there for them. I'm glad it's you."

"Thanks." Susan set the phone to silent and dropped it into her pocket.

ANDREW WAS VAGUELY aware of a ringing phone and Susan leaving. He looked up when she wandered back in. She gave Kandace a cup of coffee and a pink-frosted cookie wrapped in plastic.

"The cafeteria is closed"—Susan crossed the room and handed him coffee and a granola bar—"so I had to get vending-machine food. I'm sorry it's not fancier. You both should eat," she said.

"Yes, ma'am." Andrew forced the food down his throat, not tasting any of it, and washed it down with coffee that scalded. When it all hit his stomach, he realized how hungry he was.

Susan handed him a second bar and sat.

Kandace ate more slowly, sectioning off pieces one at a time. "Thank you."

Susan yawned wide, not masking it well with her hand. Was she on her second sleepless night, after what happened with her father? That seemed so long ago.

Andrew patted his knee. "Come here."

She shifted in her seat until she could lay her head on his leg. The warm weight helped focus his thoughts. He trailed his fingers through her hair and turned his attention back to Lucas. *Please, God. Whatever you want, let him be all right.*

Seconds turned to minutes, and Susan's breathing slowed. Andrew let her sleep. Someone should be able to get some rest. He looked at Kandace. "I can't keep leaving him after a couple of weeks. This will be my first Christmas ever with him, and it feels wrong there haven't been more."

"You can't take him back to Georgia." Kandace sounded as exhausted as he felt.

"Because it'd be selfish of me. Isn't that what you always say? The way you always get me to leave him in your hands?"

She shook her head. "He's got his friends here."

"He's got a school and a support foundation who have pushed him to think he doesn't deserve to live if he likes other boys *that way*." Andrew kept his voice low, despite the anger thrumming through him.

Kandace crumpled the empty plastic wrapper, then watched it expand, before squashing it in her fist again. "I'm not saying you need to walk away from him. I'm saying you can't take him back to Georgia with you."

"So what? I pick up and move my entire life here?"

She looked from him, to Susan, to Lucas, then back at Andrew again. "Do you really hate this town that much?"

"That's not the point. I'm established in Georgia."

"And Lucas's established here. Are you leaving friends behind? Do you have associates you can't communicate with online? You know—through your web-based business?"

He wanted to argue, but the longer the idea bounced in his head, the harder it was to ignore.

Lucas let out a croaky groan, and Andrew whirled in time to see the boy flutter his eyelids. Andrew's heart leapt into his throat, and he pushed the call button for the nurse. Kandace was on her feet, grasping Lucas's hand.

Andrew grasped Susan's shoulder. "Wake up, sleepy head."

She sat straight up. He helped her stumble to her feet, and pulled her with him as the doctor and nurse rushed into the room. They pulled the breathing tube out, ran tests, spat numbers at each other, and checked monitors over and over.

Lucas lay there, eyes closed and consciousness gone again.

The doctor turned to Kandace. "He's closer to safe. He's breathing on his own, but we need him to wake up."

She nodded.

Susan pulled Andrew's arms around her, offering more comfort than he suspected he was giving her. She felt like the closest thing to a lifeline he'd ever had, and fuck if he didn't need that.

TWENTY-TWO

LUCAS WORKED HIS EYES OPEN A SHORT TIME LATER, and rasping, "Mama?"

Andrew gasped in relief.

"I'm here, sweetie." Kandace knelt next to Lucas.

Andrew wanted the right to offer his comfort.

"I'm sorry." Tears rolled down Lucas's cheeks.

Kandace brushed them away. "You didn't do anything wrong."

"I did. I'm messed up and evil, and if I can't stop, I don't deserve to live."

Andrew clenched his fist so hard, his nails dug into his palms, but he couldn't stop.

"That's not true." Kandace stroked Lucas's cheek. "None of that is true."

Andrew couldn't do this. He crouched on the other side of the bed and took Lucas's hand. So tiny and bony. Kandace grimaced, and Lucas frowned.

"I know sometimes I embarrass you," Andrew said, "and sometimes you don't like me very much. That's okay." It wasn't, but this wasn't the time for that conversation. "Everything you are is okay. You can like what you want and who you want. That's not anyone else's business. You're an amazing, brilliant person. There's not evil anywhere in you."

Lucas's scowl deepened. "How would you know?"

"I'm a good judge of character, regardless of what that character is."

Lucas started crying again. What did Andrew say wrong?

"Mama?" His teary cry tore Andrew apart. "I don't want to go back to therapy. Don't make me, please?"

"Never. I promise." Kandace carefully helped Lucas sit and pulled him into a hug.

The next little while passed in a blur of more tests, more conversations with the doctor, and explaining to Lucas he couldn't eat until they were sure his stomach could handle it. He had to start with ice chips and work his way up.

It was close to one in the morning, when the doctor declared Lucas stable and moved him to a regular room. Lucas drifted off to sleep within moments of being settled. But this time it was a peaceful sleep, without the help of a respirator or oxygen. Only two lines ran to him now. One from the monitor on his finger, and his IV.

A lot of the stress had vanished from Kandace's face, leaving exhaustion room to sink in. There was a reclining chair near the bed. She settled into that but didn't kick back. She looked at Andrew. "We'll talk after he's discharged. I promise. Whatever the two of you want—you and him—you can have."

"All three of us decide." The pressures of the day gnawed at his edges.

"Go back to the house and get a couple of hours of sleep. Shower. All that," Kandace said.

"I can't."

"I'm staying here. All the finest accommodations." She gestured at the chair. "Lucas's okay. You'll probably be back before he wakes up. You were here when it mattered, and you will be again. Besides"—she nodded at Susan, who snoozed in a plastic seat against the wall—"you're not the only one who needs to rest and clean up."

"I'll call her a cab."

"Go home, Andrew. For a little while. There's nothing else you can do here."

He looked between Susan and Lucas. "All right. But we'll be back in the morning. I'll bring breakfast."

"Sounds great." Kandace gave him a tired smile.

SUSAN HAD STRUGGLED to stay awake as the night wore on, but now that they were back at Kandace's house, adrenaline mingled with weariness. The tree in the living room was lit up, and dozens of muddy tracks from the day's bedlam marred the light carpet.

The place was an eerie combination of warm and far too empty. As long as everyone got to come home, Susan suspected the fridge would be full of casseroles from the neighbors by tomorrow night, and someone would volunteer to help Kandace clean up.

Andrew returned from the room he said was his when he stayed here, and handed her a stack with a T-shirt on top. "So you can change into more comfortable clothes to sleep in."

"I don't know if I'm sleeping any time soon." She took the offering anyway.

Dark circles hung under his eyes, but the glower he'd worn all night had faded. "A shower might help you relax. You can use the one attached to Kandace's room, if you're interested. Wash some of the dirt off. Warm up."

"That sounds nice." She followed the direction he pointed, until she found the room in question. The master bath was done up elegantly, in frosted chrome and porcelain, with both a shower in against the wall and a free-standing tub. A bath would be amazing right now. It would probably also lull her to sleep before she was ready. Shower it was.

When she emerged, she felt infinitely more relaxed but no closer to sleep. She tugged on the T-shirt Andrew gave her, and smiled when she looked in the mirror. *Definitely one of his.* Not only did it hang halfway down her thighs, but the text across the chest read, *How do you keep a moron in suspense?*

The only other thing in the stack was a pair of cotton boxers. She pulled those on as well and wandered out into house. The dark quiet was more calming than she expected. Despite this only being her second time here, the home felt welcoming. There were two rooms on this side of the living room. The second was Lucas's, she assumed, from the smaller bed, telescope near the window, and glow-in-the-dark stars dotting the ceiling.

Andrew's room was on the other side of the house, so she made her way back there. She paused in the doorway, thoughts grinding to a halt when she saw him. His jeans hung low on his hips, and he wasn't wearing anything else. His back was to her, his attention on a dresser against the wall. Faint scars ran along one shoulder, down his back, and wrapped around his arm. Each time he moved, muscle rippled under the skin. His wet hair lay in dark curls along the back of his neck.

It was tempting to stare a little longer, but she found her voice. "Did I steal your only shirt?"

"I got distracted." He nodded at a series of framed pictures.

She moved into the room, to stand next to him. As far as she could tell, they were all photos of Lucas—as a baby, a toddler, and at various other points in his life.

"I was on the other side of the world when half of this happened." Andrew's voice was quiet. "While I was taking naked pictures, Kandace was raising this amazing boy and sending me some of the better shots. And she's got a point, the more I think about it."

"About what?"

"If I want to be in his life, I need to be here. I can't keep running away from this place."

She couldn't help but wonder if Mercy went through a similar thought process a few months ago, which reminded her of Dad. Her stomach twisted in on itself. This wasn't the time to fall back down that rabbit hole. "If you're looking for me to talk you out of it, I won't. I think it's a good idea. Besides, from a purely selfish perspective? I like your company."

He turned to look at her. He raised one brow as he dragged his gaze up her body, and her skin heated to scorching. "Spending more time with you would be a nice side-effect."

"What?" she asked when she realized he wasn't looking away.

"I'm imagining what is or isn't underneath that shirt. Wondering what it would take to get you out of it, so I can find out."

She gave him a timid smile, unsure how to respond.

"What?" He mimicked her earlier question.

"I don't know if you're teasing or serious."

"I'm completely serious." He knotted his fingers in her hair, holding her head captive. "Everything's that happened tonight has me thinking... I used to be fearless."

"Used to be?" She forced herself to speak, despite the way his intense gaze drilled into her.

He let out a strained chuckle. "You heard me. Believe it or not, I'm a *do no harm* kind of guy. After the accident all those years ago, and the events leading up to it... I'd walked away from Lucas and pissed off Mercy to the point we weren't speaking, because of what *I* wanted. I swung in the opposite direction after that. Not on purpose; it's just the way things happened."

"How do you mean?"

"I kept my distance from Lucas under the pretense of not ruining his life, but it was so I didn't have to deal with what I might do wrong if I stuck around. In the end, it didn't matter. He's caught up in a cycle of self-loathing regardless. I'm not saying he'd be better or worse if I stuck around, but at least the situation would have been honest from the start."

Susan wasn't sure what to say. She agreed but didn't think it was polite to throw that back in his face with *took you long enough*. She settled for nodding.

"Now that I know he's going to be all right, this whole realization thing is taking off on a tangent." He raked his fingers through his hair. "You look amazing, like you always do. Fresh out of the shower, covered in mud, made up for dinner with your friends—it doesn't matter. I adore you, Suzie-Q. And—fuck—I'm tired of fighting this. I don't want to lose out on whatever potential lies between us. I desperately want to strip you out of those clothes."

She didn't know if it was the tension talking, or if his words meant more. She didn't care. "Me too."

He brushed his lips over hers, and a pleasant shiver ran down her spine. When he tightened his grip, yanking back her head, she gasped. He muffled the sound, kissing her hard, gliding his tongue over her bottom lip, then further into her mouth, to dance and tease.

She didn't know how it was possible, but each time he kissed her was more intense than the last. She dug her fingers into his chest, sinking into every new sensation. The scent of his body wash. The hint of toothpaste. The hammering of his heart against her hand, beating as hard as hers. No one would interrupt them this time.

The realization tied her gut in knots, and her anticipation spiked.

"Jesus, the things you do to me." His lips hummed against her skin, as he traced them down her neck. "And you don't realize it." He trailed his palm along her arm to her hand, then moved both down his stomach. He wrapped her fingers around the bulge in his jeans, groaning when she stroked through denim. "I fantasize about your mouth wrapped around my cock." He caught her earlobe between his teeth, tugging before he let go. "What it'll feel like to bury my dick inside you. I can't get you out of my fucking head."

At least she wasn't the only one. Each time she dragged a finger along his erection, he jerked into her hand. He was big. Was that normal? "What if it doesn't fit?" She flushed, as the question slipped out.

He licked along the edge of her ear, his whisper as much breath as voice. "I promise you'll enjoy every minute of this, even when there's a little pain."

That sounded far more enticing than she'd expect. "It's a promise, huh? Be careful. You'll give me high expectations."

"Good." He raked his nails down her back, before pulling the shirt over her head. He leaned away to look her over and smirked. The way he looked at her made need clench in her belly and focus between her legs, throbbing and damp. "Pink. Noted."

"What is?"

"Your nipples. It's tough to daydream about doing this, when I can't picture them."

Before she could ask *doing what*, he lowered his head and licked one hardened nub. The coarse texture of his tongue over the sensitive skin drew a sigh. That was much more intense than her own fingers. When he wrapped his lips—warm and firm —around the area and scraped his teeth along the skin, her hips bucked.

His laugh murmured over her body. "Let's see what other buttons you have." He alternated his attentions between her breasts, sucking one while he pinched and pulled at the other. Her head grew light from the gasps and continuous pleasure, and she lost track of where one lick stopped and the next tweak started.

He moved his mouth back to hers, and the cool air danced over the dampness on her chest. His nails scraped along her hips when he hooked his thumbs in the elastic of her shorts. It only took a nudge, to send the clothing sliding to the ground.

He looked her over again. The groan that tore from his throat rolled over her and filled her floaty thoughts with promises of him doing things to her she couldn't imagine. "*Jesus Christ*. You're bald." He was focused on her crotch.

"It's a profile thing."

He joined her again, one hand at her back and the other dancing along her skin, between her navel and her mound. "You don't mean like a website profile."

She liked having this effect on him. The throaty sounds he made. The way his voice dropped every time he looked at her. "I don't wear panties under my bodysuit when I dance. The goal is minimal lines disrupting my profile."

"Fuck." He skated his fingers lower, along the edges of her thighs, and her core ached for that touch. "If you were anyone else in the entire fucking world, you'd be my sites' hottest starlet."

"But because I'm me?" An irrational fear poked up its head, asking if she wanted to know the answer.

He nudged her back, to sit on the bed. "You're all mine." As he lowered himself, he pushed her to lie back, then kissed along her chest, down her stomach, and over the top of her legs. He nudged her thighs apart and kissed up the inside of one, then down the other, never touching the wetness between. She squirmed under the attention, gripping the comforter to keep her hands from acting on their own. She ached to slide her fingers *down there* if he wouldn't. But the agony of anticipation was delicious.

He traced her lower lips with a fingertip, sliding easily over smooth, slick skin, and a new level of enjoyment jolted through her. When he followed the same path with his tongue, she gasped, and her butt rose several inches to get closer.

"You like that?" His breath was tantalizing against her skin.

She managed to force a *mhm* through her whimper.

"You taste amazing." He followed her folds, licking up. When he wrapped his lips around her aching button, she cried out and ground into his face. The first shudder of climax rolled through her, but flattened out when he eased up the pressure. For several moments, he sucked until he pushed her to the edge, then softened his touch. She squirmed under the ministrations, licking her lips to find moisture, unable to think about anything but the face buried between her legs.

He carried her to the brink again, but this time didn't back off. Orgasm gripped her, crashing over her body, flowing through her arms, and sapping the strength from her legs. She jerked away from his touch when it became too much. He moved his mouth back to hers, dancing and splaying his fingers over the outside edges of her mound.

She dove into the kiss. She'd tasted herself

before, on her own fingers. It was different on someone else's lips. Its own kind of high. As the rush started to ebb, she felt a nudge at her opening, and before she could process it, a sharp sting snapped between her legs. His finger was deeper insider her than she'd ever dared go with her vibrator. He slid it out and in again, and ecstasy mingled with the pain.

"Are you okay?" He searched her eyes.

She bit her bottom lip. "I think you broke something."

"That was the point. *Now*"—he kissed along the edge of her ear, voice a whisper—"I fuck you until you're sore and hoarse."

A chill of anticipation raced through her, and she nodded.

TWENTY-THREE

A<small>NDREW WAS BARELY AWARE OF STRIPPING OFF HIS</small> jeans then fumbling to grab a condom from the wallet he'd left on the nightstand. He unwrapped the rubber and rolled it on, mostly thanks to muscle memory. Susan lay in the middle of the bed, looking better than any fantasy, blue eyes watching his every move.

He wedged her legs apart with his knee and rested his hands on the mattress on either side of her head. She traced her palms up his arms, and he realized he was shaking. Impatience was a bitch. He ducked his head to kiss her again, fueling a new spark of desire. He knelt upright, then used one hand to guide his cock into her.

She winced when he nudged the head in.

"You okay?" he asked.

She nodded. "Keep going."

It took the last of his restraint to ease in, filling her up, sliding inside her tight, wet hole. The friction and the way her muscles twitched around him threatened to make him come. He pumped at a slow pace, measuring her responses, and letting her moans and soft cries force every other thought out of his head.

As she relaxed under him, pushing into his pelvis and matching his rhythm, he picked up speed. When he pinned her knees to her chest, she shifted her ass. She gasped as he struck inside her deep and hard. Her breath came in short bursts, then pants, as he slammed against her. He couldn't hold back any more. Each new thrust traveled from his dick and ran through his body, stealing reason and leaving need in its place.

He couldn't take his eyes off Susan. How her face screwed up in pleasure. The winces that accompanied each groan. The flutter of her eyelids, like she couldn't decide if she wanted to watch or sink into her other senses. Her pussy tightened, squeezing his shaft. He let go of one leg, to lean forward and roll a nipple between his fingers. To kiss her and steal her soft cries.

He wanted a witty comment, but all he could find was, "*Fuck.* You feel incredible."

She managed a smile. "Better than you know."

He massaged her breast and pinched the swollen nub, hammering inside her at the same time. His balls tightened, but he wasn't ready to let go yet. Dots swam in front of his eyes. She was close; he could tell from the way she milked him. He moved his mouth to her neck and sucked the tender flesh hard, to mark her.

She dug her fingers into his arms and arched her back, a scream tearing from her throat when orgasm hit her. The pressure around his cock grew, tightening and releasing in spasms, pushing him past the edge of control. He squeezed his eyes shut, and a million stars danced behind the lids when he came. He couldn't ease up yet. Not when she continued to grind against him. Not with the intense pleasure flowing through him.

The edge faded from his climax, and he slowed reluctantly and out of necessity, until he stopped.

He forced his eyes open, to see her watching him, a mischievous smirk on her full lips. "So that's sex, huh?" Her question rasped out.

"Those are the basics." He eased out slowly, letting go of her other leg Before he leaned in for another kiss. Her chest heaved and a faint shine of sweat glowed across her face and body. *Gorgeous.*

"That was a little more than basic. I know. I've seen internet porn."

"Have you?" He stripped off the condom and wrapped it in a tissue so he could throw it out. "I'd like to watch that."

"The porn? I think you've already seen it."

"No. I'd like to watch *you* watching."

Her flushed cheeks darkened further. "There's always next time."

He stood, and wobbled for a minute before catching his balance. "Wait right here." A moment later, he returned with water for her then dropped onto the bed next to her, legs refusing to support his weight any longer.

He lay on his side and patted the mattress. "Sleepy yet?"

"No." She curled up next to him and rested her forehead against his chest. "Thank you."

He didn't think anyone had ever thanked him for sex and didn't know what the appropriate reply was. He settled for draping an arm over her and planting a kiss on the top of her head.

Within a few minutes, her breathing was slow and steady, and she relaxed limply in his arms. *Asleep.* With the haze of lust fading, the real world filtered back in, along with his own words from so many years ago—courtesy of a recent reminder. *Monogamy is fine for romantics and sheep, but I'm never tying myself to only one person.* How long until he had to break Susan's heart? "I'm sorry," he whispered in the quiet room.

"Me too." She snuggled closer.

The simple reply left a sharp jabbing pain in his chest. So much for her being asleep.

ANDREW AND SUSAN made it back to the hospital
with breakfast for Kandace. Lucas complained
when he didn't get any. That was a good sign.

Susan spent half of the day flushed from memories of the night before. The light throb between her
legs was a pleasant reminder. Did what happened
show? She swore everyone was watching her. Which
was ridiculous. They were focused on Lucas, as they
should be. But *wow*. When could she and Andrew
do that again?

The problem with that question was the one it
led to. What did his muttered apology mean? She
didn't think she was supposed to hear it, and now
she was fully awake, it seemed more like a product
of her imagination than reality. That didn't sate the
dread that unfurled inside her every time she
thought about it.

Lucas bounced back quickly, now that he was
awake. By noon, the nurses let him have Jell-O and
soda. The doctor released him that evening, as long as
he promised to take it easy on the food for a couple of
days, while his stomach recovered. The final diagnosis
was that he didn't taken enough pills to do internal
damage. They took him out for so long because of his
size and the alcohol he mixed them with.

Susan liked seeing the family happy. Andrew

seemed restrained, but he looked so much lighter than twenty-four hours ago.

They got back to Kandace's and got Lucas settled. He needed rest. Kandace and Andrew promised to talk to him after he recovered a little more, about how to make sure Lucas stayed happy and sane. Kandace also swore he wouldn't have to see anyone else until they figured out the details. That seemed to sate the boy, and he passed out in his own bed a short while later.

Andrew ordered Kandace to get some sleep. She only protested for a moment before yielding. Susan and Andrew were left alone in the living room.

Andrew handed her his phone. "Do you want to text Mercy? Let her know you're okay?"

She took the device. Typing in his passcode made her smile. The sense of humor of a five-year-old sometimes. She adored it. A twinge ghosted through her when she saw the last conversation he'd had with Mercy. The note that Susan was in his room. The deception.

She pushed aside the bad memory. That was in the past. They'd moved on. She sent Mercy a quick note. *Hey. It's Susan. Checking in. Everyone's all right, including me.*

A response came seconds later. *Glad to hear it. Thanks for letting me know. Talk soon.*

She smiled, and out of habit, hit the back button to take her to the main text screen. A flash of color caught her eye, and it took her a minute to process it was a photo. "What's this?" A voice in her head screamed not to click—that she was invading his privacy—but her thumb swiped the conversation open.

"What's what? Oh. Fuck." Andrew's exclamation echoed the one in her head, as she stared at a selfie of Rissa. Or rather, of Rissa's boobs.

This wasn't what made Susan's brain grind to a screeching halt. It was the date it was sent and Andrew's reply. *I wouldn't mind you riding me.*

Now Susan knew why she' woke up alone the morning after she threw herself at him. Because if she were anyone but her, he'd fuck the hell out of her. Wasn't that how he phrased it? She looked up, to see him frowning.

She didn't have a right to be mad. They weren't dating, and he'd never made a secret of that. "Was she fun?" Susan forced herself to sound cheerful. The crack in her words told her she failed.

"She was forward."

It wasn't a real answer. Was that what he'd tell people about Susan? Or would it be a generic kind of *she was a challenge?* Would she get that much credit in one of his stories? The thought gnawed at her. It wasn't that she was angry, but she was hurt in a way she didn't like and didn't feel she had a right to be. "I'm glad you got to hook up."

"Me too." He wouldn't meet her gaze, and his

trademark bravado was missing from his voice. He'd lied to Mercy about sleeping with Susan. It was possible he was covering up the truth about Rissa.

Realization spread through Susan. It wasn't that she minded who he'd been with in the past. She was terrified of what it meant for last night. She didn't want to ask, but she had to have it defined. It felt special, but that was her assumption. "Is that what I was last night? A hookup?"

"Suzie-Q…" He trailed off.

"I'm not upset." She managed to sound normal. "I mean, in a way, my feelings are hurt, but I never had any illusions about how inexperienced I am compared to you. I know who you are. Seems like now is a good time to discuss it, so we're on the same page." Which was ridiculous. She'd already built up a relationship for her and Andrew, weaving the idea until it was part of her reality. She tried to deny it, but with the possibility of losing him staring her down, she had to admit she was hooked.

"I've told you before, I'm not *boyfriend* material. Any past disclaimers apply. Last night was really good, but that's all it was." He rubbed the back of his neck and studied the ceiling. "I consider you a good friend." He looked at her. "That doesn't have to change unless you want it to."

"Am I the only one who felt a connection?" Why couldn't she drop this? Because she'd convinced herself he felt the same as she did, and she was going to make him admit it. How childish was that?

"I adore you. But I don't do long-term. Hell, I don't think it's fair to call it any sort of term."

"Have you ever tried?"

A sympathetic smile appeared on his face. "More times than you've had boyfriends. I'd bet a lot on that."

"Which is a low blow, and you know it."

He shrugged. "I'm trying to keep this civil and pain free. I've tried real hard not to hide my intentions from you. From the start, you've known this was a friendship and nothing more."

"Things can change." Now she sounded desperate, and she hated that as much as the growing void inside.

"This is exactly what I warned you about. You're looking for an emotional link that isn't there. You don't know enough about me, to assume there could be one."

The words and casual dismissal stung. His cool delivery chipped away at her. "I know a lot more about you than you give me credit for," she said.

"*Really?*" Snideness filled the word, and a wicked twist flickered on his face before vanishing. "Like what, Ms. Observant? If you say *there's the sex stuff*, you fail."

"This is a test? Fine. Regardless of the fact you

give everyone a nickname, you never forget a face or a real name."

"A lot of people know that."

"But you do it to keep from getting attached. You hated growing up the poor kid in a rich school, so you learned the fast quip and quick jokes were the best way to shrug off cruelty and prove to people you didn't care."

"Mercy could have told you that." His wince defied his casual tone.

"She didn't. But this isn't a question of *how* I know, but *what* I know. Which includes the fact that you're a lot kinder and more compassionate than you want anyone to think, and it's not for some pseudo-macho reason. You'd surrender nearly everything, rather than hurt the people you care about." She swallowed, not sure she should say the next bit. But she was going to lay this all on the line if it was going to hurt either way. "And I know you care about me as much as I care about you."

"You're right."

Her heart leapt into her throat.

"Which is why I'll surrender you to keep from hurting you," he said.

Anger shoved her hope aside. All this discussion, so he could pull the *this is what's best for you* card? No. She wasn't having that. "That's an asshole move. You don't get to decide what is and isn't good for me. That's not your call."

"Consent goes both ways."

She hated the way he abused and tossed that line around. "Because you know what I need better than I do? You fucking hypocrite. Where the hell do you get off, pulling a line like that? Especially after last night's monologue, about how you regret pushing your will on Lucas's life."

"I was exhausted and strung out. Not thinking straight. I needed an outlet after a stressful day. What do you want me to say?"

The excuses burrowed under her skin, raising her ire to new levels. "So, like that— *bam*—this is over?"

"*This* never started. You got to slum it for a while. I had some fun. Time to move on."

"That's how you sum up our time together."

He nodded at the phone in her hand. "Call your sister. Tell her to come get you. You can leave that on the coffee table when you're done."

She itched to chase after him when he walked out of the room, but her pride didn't need another blow. If he was going to be a stubborn asshole, she'd let him. Tears stung her eyelids, and she wiped them away angrily. If this was how he approached romance, he was right. She was better off without him.

TWENTY-FOUR

ANDREW HATED HIMSELF MORE WITH EACH WORD HE used, to push Susan away. He meant what he said last night, but it was idealistic bullshit. He saw her hurt today, when she found the exchange with Rissa, and reality crashed in. If he stayed in Susan's life, it would crush them both. Her, when he fucked up, and him as a result.

Better a little pain now, than a screaming blow-out a month or two down the line.

She was a fascination, unique and compelling. Once he got used to her, his interest would wander. It always did. A shout in the back of his mind repeated, *What if this time is different?* He never managed to shut the question up completely, but if he threw himself into other things, he could ignore the echoes.

For the next several days, he helped Kandace

make sure Lucas was recovering. Andrew wasn't surprised Mercy refused to take his calls. He left her a message, saying he was going to work from Kandace's for the rest of his trip. A few hours later, a courier showed up with his laptop and a note from Mercy, letting him know they could conduct any other meetings via phone or Skype, the way they did when he wasn't in town.

Would he be able to win back Mercy's trust this time? The question tried to summon another one—how long until he got over Susan. He ignored both.

That night, six days after bringing Lucas home, Andrew and Kandace sat at the kitchen table to figure out what came next for them.

"After Christmas, I'll fly back to Georgia long enough to tie up loose ends and grab my things," Andrew said.

Kandace smiled. She hadn't done much of that lately, and it was nice to see. "It'll be nice to finally have you close again. It's a shame it took this much to get you here."

"Mom." Lucas stood in the doorway, shuffling his weight from one foot to the other. "Can I talk to you?"

Andrew pushed back from the table. "We can wrap this up later." He was trying his damnedest to not push his presence on Lucas—assuring the boy there was no reason to call him *Dad*; making sure it was clear Lucas didn't have to talk to him unless he wanted to… Lucas took full advantage of the offer and kept his distance from Andrew.

"Both of you." Lucas's voice was so soft, Andrew wasn't sure he heard right.

Andrew sat back down and clenched his jaw shut, terrified of saying the wrong thing and obliterating this opportunity.

"I don't want to go back to school after winter break," Lucas said.

"At all, or just that school?" Kandace's tone was calm and unwavering. It carried no judgement or anger.

Andrew was impressed. Would he need to learn to do that?

Lucas continued to study his feet. "I need to learn stuff still. But I don't like it there."

"We'll find you a different school. Do you want to sit with us?" Kandace gestured to a chair, toeing it out from the table a few inches.

Lucas shook his head. "No, thank you. I'm going to my room, to read." He stayed in the doorway, though.

"What's wrong?" Kandace asked.

"Are you really moving here? Like, for good?" Lucas looked at Andrew.

This was an easy enough question to answer. "Yup. There's a house a few blocks away I'm trying to buy." Andrew put an offer in a few days ago.

"I don't have to live there, do I?"

"No. But you're welcome any time." Andrew could do this. He could be a normal, reasonable uncle figure about the entire thing.

Silence descended over the room again. Lucas fiddled with his fingers, looking everywhere but at the table.

Maybe Andrew couldn't do this. Silence wasn't his thing, and neither was beating around the bush. He'd been aching to broach the subject of what happened to Lucas and the best way to work toward recovery. "Would you like to talk to someone about what happened in therapy?" That was as nonjudgmental as he could be with the question.

"*No.*" Lucas's voice cracked.

Kandace gripped her mug so hard, her knuckles turned white.

"I don't want to talk to you, because you'll make fun of me," Lucas said.

Andrew squelched the hurt the words caused and forced himself to stay calm. He wasn't sure what he'd done to earn this level of scorn, but he'd work as hard as he could, to get past it. "I never want to make fun of anything that hurts you. And I didn't mean me. Someone who specializes in listening." He'd gotten a few referrals for local shrinks who specialized in child psychology and sexual identity.

"I'm not going to therapy again. Don't make me." Tears welled up in Lucas's eyes.

Fuck.

Kandace crossed the room and crouched to pull him into a hug. "I won't, sweetie. I promised, and I meant it. That's not what he means."

Technically, that was exactly what Andrew meant, but he understood why phrasing was important. "This isn't someone who wants to change you. They just listen. You can even take your mom with you, but you don't have to."

"I don't know. Maybe. I'm going to bed now, if that's okay."

Kandace hugged him again and pointed him toward his room. "Of course. Good night, sweetie."

The next day, Lucas announced he wanted to talk to someone. Andrew tried to mimic Kandace's calm smile, but inside he was cheering and hopeful.

ANDREW DOVE back into the piles of work waiting for him—contracts to be signed, decisions to be made. Working from Kandace's was far less of a distraction than being in the R&T offices.

Through it all, Andrew kept Susan out of his mind. He spent lunches and evenings getting to know Lucas. It wasn't a smooth relationship. The boy frequently didn't want anything to do with him.

And when it was night and quiet, a smiling face taunted Andrew's memories. Susan's crystalline laugh and clear blue eyes haunted his dreams. He needed to move on. This was a great time to evaluate how the market was changing. Which sites needed to go. What new fetishes were trending.

Could Susan bend into positions like that?

God-Fuck-It.

You're being a Grade-A jackass about this. The taunting echoed in his thoughts.

Nope. Not listening. He had porn to evaluate. It had been a week and a half since he saw her. Why wouldn't she leave his thoughts alone?

Conversations were terse with Mercy. That hurt, but at least she was taking his calls again. She'd recover, he'd find a new fascination, and they'd go back to normal.

"How's Susan?" The question slipped out at the end of a business meeting, and he snarled at himself.

"None of your fucking business."

That seemed fair. "Right. I'll let you go. If I don't talk to you in the next couple of days, Merry Christmas."

She sighed. "Why did you do it?"

That was such an open-ended question, he didn't know where to start. "Why haven't you hung up on me yet?"

"I don't know," she said.

Because you adore me, stuck in his throat. Probably

not the best time for playful teasing. "I'll take what I can get, regardless of your reasons."

"You led her on, and then you were an asshole about it." Mercy's anger singed him over the phone lines.

He wanted to argue he hadn't done anything like that, but while he told a lot of stories, he didn't want this situation misunderstood. Susan was more than a fascination. He felt like shit without her around, missed her, and cared about her so much, he was willing to risk an incredible friendship, to tell her how he felt. "I'm sorry," he said.

"I don't believe you."

The words hurt more than he expected. "What are the odds you'll give me her new number?" Stupid question. There was no way. He needed to talk to Susan, though. Ignoring what he felt for her hurt too much. Even if she didn't forgive him, he needed to tell her she was right about how he felt.

"How soon do you think Hell will freeze over?"

Her response meant he wasn't the only one guilty of imposing his will on Susan's best interests. "I just want to tell her I was wrong. You can't stop me from talking to her." Not the best approach to take. What the fuck was wrong with him?

"That doesn't mean I have to make it easy," she said.

"That's not your call."

She gave a barking laugh. "You're one to talk.

How's it feel to be on the other side of that line? I won't let you do to her what you did to me. Walk away now, and maybe we can repair our friendship."

The possibility of losing Mercy slammed into him. He didn't expect to have to choose between his anchor and the woman he was falling for. "I'll leave you both alone, but you have to do something for me in return."

"You've used up all your favors."

"I want one more anyway. Promise to tell Susan I asked about her. You don't have to pass along a message or tell her what we talked about, or that you're being as stubborn as I was about what's best for her. Just tell her I asked."

"It won't change anything, but I'll tell her. Goodbye."

He stared at the phone for several minutes after, replaying everything in his head. Not only the conversation, but the time since he' arrived in Utah. The bits with Susan and without.

If Susan called him back, would he sacrifice his friendship with Mercy to tell Susan how he felt?

Yes. The admission hurt. He hoped it didn't come down to that. Mercy would pass along his message; he didn't doubt it. But how long could he force himself to wait, to see if Susan called back, before he broke, drove up there, and demanded to see her?

He'd surrendered that right, but he wanted one more chance to admit he'd fucked up.

SUSAN KNEW THIS WAS COMING. Andrew never made any secrets about it. He tried to warn her up front that she'd get emotionally attached to her first time. She insisted she knew better. How naïve was that?

For the first couple of days, she didn't want to leave her room. She lay in bed, staring at the ceiling and wondering why tears wouldn't come if it hurt this badly. She forced herself up on Friday. She had an interview to go to and a life to lead. A ghosted memory of a mistake wouldn't take that from her.

Driving into Salt Lake so close to Christmas was a pain. Traffic everywhere. People. Snow. But it was worth it. She nailed the classroom portion of her interview. The kids loved her, and she had a blast instructing them. A happy elation filled her when she got the job, but she couldn't find the energy to celebrate.

She spoke with her Academic Adviser at the college. It took a little convincing to drive home the point that no, she wasn't going to school on her dad's dollar anymore. The guy was sympathetic when he finally got it. He helped her fill out financial aid forms based on her new job. She'd have to skip the spring term, because she needed pay stubs to finish her paperwork. He promised to push her application through, the moment he was able to. That gave her another couple of years, until graduation, to figure out how she'd pay the bill.

Phone call completed, she wandered into the kitchen. Mercy was home. Susan could only take so many pity looks and weak smiles.

"How are you doing?" It was the same question Mercy always led with, these days.

Susan had a prepackaged answer, as well. "Fine." She grabbed the carton of orange juice from the fridge.

"Andrew asked about you."

The juice slipped from her hand and hit the floor with a plastic *splat*. She fumbled to retrieve it and set it back on its shelf. "Oh?"

"I told him I'd tell you that."

Susan turned to face her. "Should I call him?"

Mercy hesitated, studying the counter. "That's not up to me."

"Did you and he ever..." She couldn't ask that. It was the last thing she wanted to hear.

"Dated? Slept together? Both."

That didn't hurt the way Susan thought it would. She expected it. "What happened?"

"He wanted an open relationship. I didn't."

"So he cheated on you?" The possibility bothered Susan, but it didn't sound right.

"No. He told me from the start. I thought I was okay with it, and I wasn't."

"Do you ever regret it? The breaking up bit."

"I don't. I've always loved Ian. Andrew knew that before I did."

"And Andrew?"

"I don't know that he's ever loved someone before now."

Before now. The words chewed at Susan, making her decision more difficult. Everything he did to push her away infuriated her—treating her like she couldn't think for herself, turning away after she laid her feelings out on the line... Was he capable of admitting he made a mistake? Mercy only said he mentioned her. Not that he apologized or asked for anything specific. Was Susan a booty call now?

"Before I forget." Mercy touched her arm, drawing her attention again. "We're having Christmas dinner with Liz. You're invited, and we'd love to have you along."

That was what Susan needed. Rather than watching two people swoon over each other on their first holiday together, she could watch five. "Thanks, but I'll hang out here, if that's okay."

"Of course it is." Mercy's frown said it wasn't quite. "It's an open offer, if you change your mind."

TWENTY-FIVE

Kandace stood in the dining room doorway, dressed in her Sunday best. "You sure you'll be okay while I'm gone?"

"I'm fine," Lucas said.

"I'll only be out for a few hours." She kissed him on the cheek.

Andrew rolled his eyes at the display, but he liked seeing it as much as he liked that Lucas had decided Andrew was an acceptable substitute for Midnight Mass. This was one of several nice surprises since the boy started talking to someone who understood him and was equipped to help him embrace what made him happy. "Go. Worship. He's kicking my ass." Andrew gestured at the Monopoly board on the table. "I'm going to have him negotiate the rest of this house purchase."

"He gets the standard three percent if he does that." Kandace turned toward the front door. "Have fun, boys."

Andrew rolled the dice, then moved his car to land on St. Charles Place.

Lucas held out his hand. "Pay up."

"Or I put you to bed before Santa gets here."

"I'm ten. I don't believe in Santa."

Lucas was starting to loosen up around him. Andrew saw the trepidation still, but they had time. "You left milk and cookies out."

"So I could sneak out here and eat them after you passed out. Pay up."

Andrew counted out the rent for the hotel-laden square. He couldn't believe he was losing at Monopoly, to a ten-year-old. Pride bristled inside. "You're not eating all those alone. You're sharing."

"All right." Lucas grabbed the plate off the counter, a second one from the cupboard, and separated one cookie from the stack. He handed it over.

"Thanks. So generous."

Lucas held up the stack of fake money. "You're short on your rent. Extra cookies are for people who pay the bills."

"I need a little more time. I'm almost at *Go*."

"It's on the other side of the board."

Andrew laughed. "All right. You win. Do you want to play again?"

"You're not tired of getting your butt kicked?"

"Incredibly."

Lucas sank into his seat, grin fading into a more contemplative look. He took a bite of cookie and chewed slowly, swallowing before he spoke. "Where's my biological mom?"

Andrew was grateful to hear the question phrased this way, rather than *real mom*. That didn't mean he looked forward to sharing the truth. Was there a delicate way to put *she didn't want you*? Especially to a kid who was recovering from a brainwashing that told him he was worthless. "She decided you needed a better life than she could give you, and she asked Kandace to take on her role."

"Why did you wait so long to tell me?"

"I didn't know before you were born. Your birth mother didn't tell me she was expecting. I found out when Kandace called me, and by then, I was in another continent. She'd always wanted kids and couldn't have them, and she was going to be so much better at raising you than I would be."

"So why change your mind now?"

Andrew sighed. "Wouldn't you rather find out now, than ten or twenty years down the line? If you think the resentment is bad today…"

"I don't resent you," Lucas said, "but I do wonder why she didn't want me and neither do you."

"I want to be able to call you my son. I don't always make the right decisions, but I thought I was doing what was best for you." The words echoed in Andrew's head. Not that this was the same as the situation with Susan. Lucas had been an infant; choices had to be made on his behalf. But Susan... Andrew shook away the thought. The conversation at hand was too important to be distracted from. "I'm here now. We can't go back, but I'm hoping we can move forward."

"I guess." Lucas shrugged. Instead of laying out the board again, he started putting the pieces away. "When is Susan coming to visit again?"

"You know what? Let's go watch *It's a Wonderful Life*."

"You told Mom you hate that movie."

He did. It was sappy and sugary and everything he usually wanted to avoid thinking about. "I exaggerated."

"You do that a lot. But okay." They finished, put the box back in its closet, and settled on the couch, to watch TV.

Next thing Andrew knew, someone was shaking him awake. "Come on. It's present time," Lucas said.

Andrew forced his eyes open, to find a clock. "It's five in the morning."

"Welcome to parenthood." Kandace sat in the chair across from him, a dry smile on her face.

For a while, Andrew watched them open presents, until a pile of colored paper littered the floor, replacing the pretty boxes that had been under the tree. He enjoyed watching every single minute of it. A year ago, he wouldn't have thought this possible.

The scene wasn't complete, though. A longing he refused to name chomped behind his ribs, begging for attention. How long until that feeling faded?

By ten, Lucas was asleep again, curled up in in a different chair, wrapped in a new bathrobe, and hugging the toy he insisted he was too old for.

"I'm going out for a little bit." Andrew needed to clear his head. See if he could shake this lingering… whatever.

"Dinner's at four."

"Got it. I'll be back."

He didn't know where he was headed, but the lack of traffic in town was nice. The occasional car passed on a cross street, and that was it. There were a few more vehicles on the freeway, heading into the mountains. People coming or going over the pass, to see family.

Mercy and Ian's home was only a few blocks away. Andrew's brain screamed for him to turn around and go back to Kandace's. His brain hadn't been his best ally lately. Maybe it was time he let his heart have a say. He pointed the SUV toward their place.

No cars sat in the driveway, but they were most

likely in the garage. He steeled himself to have the door slammed in his face, and made his way to the house. Christmas lights twinkled through slits in the curtains, but no other light or movement caught his eye. He knocked and waited.

Then he rang the bell.

Then hammered the side of his fist against the door.

They might be avoiding him, but it wasn't like Mercy or Ian. No one was home. The acceptance filled him with a heavy disappointment. *Now what?*

Get in the car and drive again. It was better than sitting on the front porch of an empty home, freezing his ass off.

He didn't realize what his destination was, until he turned down a familiar side street. It led to the clearing where he took Susan the other day. Had it been two weeks? It seemed so long ago.

Someone had beaten him there. A familiar battered Honda sat near the tree line. It was Mercy's car, but the woman standing near the guardrail—blue hair barely brushing her ears, with dark roots showing through—definitely wasn't Mercy.

Susan.

His heart slammed into his ribs, thudding so hard it rattled his skull. This was either his second chance or fate's way of fucking with him a little more before it ripped him apart. He hesitated.

Could he do this? He had to. He didn't deserve another chance to make things good with her, but he wasn't going to waste it.

Susan didn't move when he pulled in. Didn't look up when he parked. Kept her gaze fixed on whatever held her attention when he got out of the SUV.

Please, God, let me get this right.

SUSAN WAS LOST IN THOUGHT. Spending Christmas with Mercy for the first time in ten years was wonderful. Mercy tried one more time to get Susan to join them at Liz's, but Susan wasn't part of that circle. It didn't feel right to join in. It hurt to not have the rest of the family here, but not so much she could forgive what Dad said. She'd called her brothers and sister, and all made it clear she wasn't welcome in their lives or around their children. After the way they treated Mercy, Susan wasn't surprised, but that didn't make it hurt any less.

And she wasn't going to call Andrew, as much as she wanted to. Did she have a problem with him seeing other people if they dated? She'd picked it all apart until her mind chased in circles. She loved his stories. Hearing about the things he'd done was a massive turn-on. Seeing it might not be the same. There was no jealousy over his past, but there was a little envy she hadn't experienced those things. She didn't care he'd gone and picked up Rissa; it bothered her that he kept it a secret. That it happened the same night he turned Susan down. That he used it as an excuse to push her away instead of owning up to his real feelings.

All that pondering brought her back here, in spite of herself. She was vaguely aware of the tires crunching behind her and a car door opening and closing, but her thoughts had greater hold of her than the world around her did.

Her heart skipped when the soft strains of a song reached her ears, delivered in a seductive tenor. "Her smiles, her frowns, her ups, her downs are second nature to me now, like breathing out and breathing in."

The song was from *My Fair Lady*. The voice was Andrew's. She knew it without looking. She stared into the canyon below, unsure what she was supposed to say. She was torn between kissing him and telling him to go to Hell. Either way, she'd make a fool of herself.

"I don't get any applause?" he asked.

She crossed her arms, more to keep herself in check than anything.

"One of the things I love most about this place is the solitude. If you want that, tell me and I'll leave." The playfulness faded from his voice, but the kindness lingered.

She clenched her jaw and dug her fingers into her arms, to keep from reacting.

"I'll go away anyway, if you're not going to look at me. But I'm going to tell you what I'm thinking first." He paused for several seconds. "No answer? That's fair. I've never met anyone like you. From that very first night, you looked past everything I am, to peer into my soul. Which is really kind of terrifying. I've got a lot of shadows and skeletons lurking in there. It never mattered how much you saw; you didn't flinch. You wanted to know more, but not to judge."

A raw sensation clawed at her throat, and she wanted to ask what his point was. She wouldn't give him that satisfaction.

"I know that's who you are. You didn't do that for me, because I'm special," he said.

She choked back the *but you are* that struggled to be heard.

He sighed. "We made a connection, and it goes deeper than friendship and sex. It's exactly what you said the other day, and that's how I know I'm not the only one who feels it."

That snapped her control. She whirled and stalked toward him. "Of course I feel that way. You don't have to be a good guesser, to figure it out. I *told* you, and you pushed me out anyway. Wrapped the rejection in the same stupid bullshit everyone feeds me—*it's for your own good*. When I called you on it, you lied to my face and told me you didn't care.

"And I know you lied, because that's the one thing you do that I'll never be okay with. I don't care who you've slept with. I don't care whose pictures you drool over, or if you jerk off five times a day to your own porn or financial statements. Hell, somewhere down the line, if there was an *us*, I might be all right with us exploring with other people.

"But you know what's not all right? That you shut me out every time you're afraid of getting hurt, and then you blame it on me. Like I'm the one who can't handle it. You're the one not coping. And yeah —okay—caring about the people around you takes time to figure out, when you've ignored it your whole life. There's no magic switch to flip that says, *I'm no longer emotionally repressed.* But you're not trying. You're happy shoving all that guilt into a tiny little box, where it devours you."

She resisted the urge to draw in a large breath when the rant was finished. "You quit drinking. You gave up the painkillers. Your new addiction is self-martyrdom."

"And you," he said.

She ground her teeth together. "Wrong. This isn't where you get to be cute and seductive, so I forget what I'm talking about. I *love* you, and that might be stupid of me, and it's probably not fair, since you warned me not to fall. Perhaps in a few weeks or months or years, 'it'll fade into less than a sharp stabbing pain in my heart that makes it hard to focus on anything else, and I'll find someone new. You were right about one thing—I *do* deserve better. Better than an asshole who feels the same way about me but refuses to let himself admit it, because *ow that hurts.*"

He stared at her. Could he hear her heart hammering? Tears pricked her eyelids again. She'd exposed her soul, and she got nothing in response. Was he prepping another joke tucked inside a weak compliment?

"You're right." When he spoke, relief crashed through her. "About all of it. You nailed it. Except I haven't jerked off five times a day since I was a teenager. Dick gets raw."

She raised her brows and pursed her lips. She hated that he went for the crude punchline, but adored it at the same time, because he was still him.

He moved closer, and stopped inches away. His heat radiated toward her, carrying his comforting scent.

She could touch his face without stretching. She swallowed the lump in her throat, and clenched her hands by her sides until her knuckles ached.

He didn't reach for her. "I shouldn't have turned this all back on you. I've known so many people in my life, and you're one of the few who has any idea what she wants. You seize it. You don't back down. And you don't let anyone tell you you can't have it, no matter how many *I care about you* excuses they wrap it in. Because, if they get it—if they get you—they won't ask you to stop. I didn't want to see how I feel about you. Admitting it's there opens me up, and I don't like being exposed. Not like this, anyway." The corners of his mouth twitched.

She had to fight her smile.

He cupped her cheek and dragged his thumb along her skin. The shock and warmth made her gasp. He stroked tiny circles. "Give us a chance—give me another chance—and it'll be worth it. For me, as much as it is for you. Because what you're most right about is that I do love you. I don't know where it came from, but fuck if the feeling isn't going away. Not that I want it to. I miss you when I can't touch you or see you, or simply hear your voice."

This time, she didn't fight the desire to kiss him. She sought out his lips with hers, tentative and soft. He tightened his grip on the back of her neck and held her close, claiming her mouth. She whimpered against him, slid her hands beneath his jacket, and molded her body to his. He wrapped an arm around her waist, drew his fingers up her back under her sweater, and kissed her again and again. When he broke away, her lips were swollen, and her head was light, and she loved it.

"You're still an asshole," she said.

"I always will be." He traced a finger over her bottom lip. "So my sister is making dinner. If Thanksgiving is any indication, she'll make way too much for three people, and it'll be amazing. That is, if you're free."

"It sounds wonderful."

He nodded at the car. "Loaner?"

"Ian has been pestering Mercy to upgrade for months. He bought her a car for Christmas, so I got this one."

"It was a piece of junk when she bought it."

"Don't insult the Honda," Susan said in warning. "It's mine, and I may not have completely earned it, but I love it."

He grinned and kissed her again. "Yes, ma'am. Think it'll hold out on the drive to Salt Lake?"

"It depends. Do you plan on finding another excuse to tell me off, so I'm stranded down there if I don't bring my own ride?"

ANDREW COULDN'T IGNORE his hurt at the comment, but he deserved it. "No. In fact, it's going to be tough to let you out of my sight for the next couple of days." Or weeks. Or months.

"I'll drop the car off at Mercy's and ride down with you. Are you flying home after Christmas?"

"Yes." Inspiration struck. It was time to push his luck a little further.

Her face fell. "You decided not to stay with Lucas after all?"

He kissed the corners of her mouth and then her pouty bottom lip. "Exactly the opposite."

"Which means…?"

He told her about the house he' made the offer on, and that he'd return to Georgia to collect some of his stuff, then come back here. He watched her smile slip back on as he spoke. He loved this look and the way her eyes lit up. "And my question is— what are you doing next week?"

"Sitting around the house, staring at the wall?"

"Fly back with me. We'll load up a U-Haul. Take our time driving back here. Test out a couple of hotel rooms along the way. If you're going to expand your horizons, hotel sex is in a category of its own."

"Because you're never sure how many other people have screwed on those sheets?" she asked flatly.

He saw the teasing underneath. He leaned close to her ear and murmured, "And everyone who hears you screaming when you come knows exactly what you're doing. So when you run into the guy next door in the hall, the next morning, you can wink and smile and say you hope he slept well the night before."

She smacked his arm. "Is that supposed to be alluring?"

"Tell me it's not."

"In a twisted kind of way, it is." She kissed him again. This felt right and amazing.

"Is that a *yes*?"

"Yes. It sounds like a blast."

"Dinner awaits, my lady." He gestured to her car. She turned away, and he pulled her back in for one more kiss. "And cream pie for dessert."

She flushed and melted against him. "You're horrible."

"And you love it."

A default text chime clashed with the peace of the clearing, and Susan reached for her purse.

"Are you really going to get that?" He tried to keep the playful tone.

"If it's Mercy—and it will be; she's the only one who has this number—she'll worry if I don't answer."

He could tell she was pleased to say that. "You should answer, in that case," he said.

She pulled up the note on her phone, and her frown grew as she read.

"What's up?"

"*Making sure you're all right,*" she read aloud. "*Dad left a message with Ian. He wants to talk to you.*"

Andrew couldn't find a response.

"Tell him he has my email address." She talked as she typed.

It was as good a response as any. "You okay?" He ran a hand along her arm, to grasp her hand.

"I will be. I just... What do I say to him?"

Andrew had a list of suggestions. "I can't tell you that. But whatever it is, it'll be the right thing."

TWENTY-SIX

S<small>USAN GRIPPED</small> A<small>NDREW'S HAND MORE TIGHTLY AND</small> pulled him into Mercy's house. He tried to tell himself what happened next wasn't a big deal, but it would hurt if things didn't go well. Not just him— he was more worried about the impact it would have on Susan.

"Hello?" Susan called.

"Kitchen." Mercy's reply carried through the house.

Andrew followed Susan toward the noise. Mercy's back was to them when they entered the room. "How's Olivia?" she asked, fiddling with the coffee maker.

It was about ten, the day after Christmas. The night before, Susan sent Mercy a generic *staying with a friend* text, to keep her from worrying, but this relationship wasn't something Susan or Andrew wanted to hide.

"I don't know. I didn't see her," Susan said.

Mercy turned their way. "I thought..." She trailed off when she met Andrew's gaze. She looked at their clasped hands, then back at their faces. "Are you fucking kidding me?"

"There's something we need to tell you." Susan squeezed his hand again.

If she did that too many more times, she'd cut off the circulation. Andrew might prefer that to this awkwardness.

Mercy didn't look at her sister. "Can we talk alone, Andrew?"

"No," Susan said. "This is about him and me, and we're both going to be here for this conversation."

"Exactly," Andrew said. They'd agreed this was what they wanted to do, and he was glad to hear her stick to the resolution.

"You're lucky Ian's out getting coffee. He might not be as generous as me." Mercy crossed her arms. "But I'm listening."

Andrew wanted to point out she probably wasn't. Not with a posture like that. However, he preferred not to aggravate her more than was necessary. "I've given Susan my apologies, and I'm lucky she heard me out. I'm sorry I promised you something I wasn't capable of doing, but I can't keep my distance from her. I have no interest in doing so. I love your sister."

Mercy laughed bitterly. "Do you even know what that means?"

He couldn't ignore the sting her words caused. "*Love?* Not in a tangible, put-it-in-a-box kind of way, but I'm figuring it out in all its various flavors."

"Don't pull a Dad." Warning filled Susan's voice.

Mercy looked at her. "Excuse me?"

"Don't walk into this, thinking you know what's best for me because of your preconceived notions. Don't project your feelings on me because you never dealt with the way you and he left things."

That wasn't the way Andrew wanted this to go.

Mercy straightened, lines creasing her brow. "You don't know anything about that."

"I know what you told me."

Andrew wasn't going to let this conversation deteriorate into bickering, and he would do everything in his power to keep from driving Mercy and Susan apart. He stepped forward, watching Mercy. "I've never said this, and I always wish I had. What happened with you and me? It was a mistake."

A shadow crossed Mercy's face.

He pushed forward before he could talk himself out of it. "Am I wrong?"

"No."

"Back then, I never should have pushed you into

a romance. But you shouldn't have told me you were okay with an open relationship when you weren't. We both fucked up, and it wasn't meant to be." The words had been in his thoughts for so long, it felt odd to hear them spoken aloud. It lifted a weight from him.

Mercy chewed the inside of her lip. "You knew I wasn't all right with it, and you plowed ahead anyway."

"True. That's kind of a cop-out, though. Don't you think? Shifting all the blame to me?" They'd never had this conversation. She refused to hear his apology back then, and the next time they spoke was when he was in the hospital. Talking about their failed romance seemed inconsequential, compared to his recovering from third degree burns. "I'll admit I had a hand in it. Hence the *we both fucked up*."

"I don't want to see the same thing happen to Susan," Mercy said. "Whatever you've told her, at least someone can benefit from my mistake."

"Do you really think it was a mistake?" Susan's question startled Andrew.

Mercy sighed. "No. It hurt, and I hated everything that came after, but I wouldn't do it differently."

"He never lied to you."

"No." Mercy shook her head. "But he did know better."

"We've established that. Here's the thing—I'm not you." Susan spoke with a simple kindness that defied the situation. "I'd like to think I'm walking into this eyes wide open. Maybe that's not true. It could be that a month or more down the line, Andrew and I realize this isn't working. But I don't expect that. Either way, you got to live your life. Allow me the same."

Andrew let go of Susan's hand, to step around the kitchen counter and approach Mercy. "I'm sorry I hurt you back then. I would have done anything to take that back and make things right between us. That's still pretty much true now, with one exception. If you make me choose you or Susan... You're my best friend, but I love her completely."

Mercy's laugh caught him off-guard.

"What?" he asked.

"The day you texted me, after my honeymoon, and I picked Susan up from your hotel, I asked her not to make me choose between the two of you. I didn't expect to have it turned back on me."

"How's it feel?" Susan teased.

Some of the tension in the room evaporated. Mercy studied Susan and then Andrew. "You look really happy. Like, genuinely."

"We are, but I'll be happier if you don't have any complaints about the situation. They won't change anything, but I'd rather not lose you." Andrew held his arms open.

Mercy hugged him tight. "Me too. But"—she hovered her mouth near his ear—"I'll still skin you alive if you make my baby sister cry."

"No, you won't." Susan's voice was firm. "I can take care of that myself."

Andrew backed up, mock horror on his face. "Whoa. No one's making me-skin rugs."

Susan and Mercy laughed. Andrew looked between them. For the first time since Mercy left him in Brazil, he didn't see any obstacles to repairing their friendship.

He studied Susan.

Yup. This was the direction he wanted his life to go.

Four days later, Andrew and Susan stopped at a hotel in Indianapolis. Her father never got back to her, after she conveyed her message to Mercy. In a way, it stung, but for the most part, Susan wasn't surprised.

The drive up from Atlanta was gorgeous. She snapped pictures the entire way. Andrew wanted to know why; she'd seen large parts of this trip before.

This was different. It felt is if she was actually living it, instead of flying into a city, visiting the hotspots, then leaving—all on a fixed schedule.

He tossed their bags next to the bed, and she moved to take a picture of him with her phone.

"No." He grabbed her wrist.

She pouted and twisted out of his grip, then snapped a shot anyway.

He snatched the camera. "My turn." A heavy current ran through his teasing.

"I don't need pictures of myself." She laughed and grabbed for the device, but he backed away.

"These, you'll want. Or I want them." His meaning sank in, and a tingle raced over her skin.

"And so will everyone else?" she asked playfully.

"No. These are for us alone."

She liked the possession in his voice and couldn't resist pushing a little more. "What if I begged you to share?"

"I like the thought of you begging. I *really* like the idea that you're an exhibitionist. But I can't stand the thought of sharing you with anyone. Maybe a way down the road, when we know each other better. *Maybe.* For now, I'm going to be really fucking selfish and keep you all for me."

"I'm good with that."

"Now that we have negotiations out of the way..." He settled a hand on her hip and guided her to stand at the foot of the bed. He stepped back several feet. "Take off your top."

His command lodged inside her, raising her temperature and making her pulse race. He snapped the first picture as she grabbed the hem of her shirt. Part of her said this should stop; it was embarrassing. It was more of a turn-on, though. Her nipples were hard in anticipation. Doing this for the camera, even with him as the photographer, was different than him simply seeing her naked.

She glided her hands up her sides as she stripped off her Tee, then tossed it aside.

"Jeans next." He clicked the button, and the digital shutter sound filled the room. His attention alternated between the phone screen and her.

She spun and shimmied out of her pants, shaking her butt at him in the process, and kicked them toward the growing pile. She turned back to face him, feeling both self-conscious and completely turned on, in nothing but her bra and panties. She licked her lips. Dampness grew between her legs.

"Play with your tits."

She reached behind her to unhook her bra.

"No. Through the fabric."

She liked this game. The lace was rough against her fingertips, and the padding underneath soft against her breasts. She whimpered at the contrasting sensations. Kneaded and massaged, desire tightening in her gut and tingling between her legs.

It felt like ages but was only a few minutes of pictures and the delicious sensation of his gaze, before he said, "*Now* the bra can come off. Slowly."

She took her time unhooking the clasps and dragging the straps down her arms. The cool air hit her chest, shocking against the warmth, and she clenched her thighs together.

"Pinch your nipples."

She obliged, tugging and twisting, sending spikes of pleasure flowing over her. She swayed her hips in time with her touch.

"Fuck. I love watching you." He dragged out the words. "Are you wet?"

She nodded.

"I want to hear you say it."

"I'm so wet." Words that sounded awkward in her head made her mouth dry and her fingers twitch with want when she spoke them.

"Do you play with yourself a lot?"

"Yes." She liked admitting that. It was wicked, and the way he dragged his gaze over her made her feel wanted.

"Show me. Strip off your panties, lie on the bed, and spread yourself wide. I want to see that gorgeous bald pussy and your fingers sliding over it, while you tell me about how you get off."

She shed the rest of her clothing and followed his orders. The click of the camera when she opened her legs drove her wild. "The night of the wedding, after you told me that first story, I went home and wore out my vibrator."

"Mmm." His groan slid through her. "I fucking love that. Show me."

She spread herself open, each shutter click pulsing against through her. She stroked slowly, wanting to drag the moment out.

"Don't hold back. Make yourself come."

"If you insist." She zeroed in on the source of her need and traced tiny circles as climax built inside, drawing her closer to the edge. Hurling her over.

She arched her back when she came, gasping and moaning.

ANDREW MEANT to stay hands off. Taking the pictures was fun, but he needed to be inside Susan. Her glistening pussy teased and called to him. He set the phone aside, unzipped his jeans, and put on a condom. She was lost in the throes of orgasm when he knelt between her legs and thrust inside her. She cried out and clenched around him.

He didn't move for a moment, both to let her slide back from the edge of pleasure and to keep from blowing his wad too soon. When she focused on him, eyes bright and clear, he rolled onto his back, pulling her on top to straddle him.

"I like this." She gave a small giggle. "New position."

"I'm having too much fun watching you. I want to see you ride me." He slid his palms up her chest, over her ribs, and to her breasts. When he tweaked her nipples, she groaned.

She rode him, matching his slow pace without pause. She reached behind her and caressed his sack. Her fingers, slick with her juices, slipped over the sensitive skin, and he clenched, trying to keep control. He could return that favor. He pressed his thumb against her clit, and she squirmed away.

"It's too much."

"Trust me." He didn't ease up.

She screamed when she came the second time, squeezing his cock and rocking against him, face screwed up in ecstasy. Electricity flowed through him, lighting up his senses and drawing out his orgasm until he climaxed hard, pounding inside her.

He hated to extract himself from the tangle of limbs, to clean up. The moment he could, he dropped back to the mattress and pulled her close. It turned out he loved the cuddling after as much as he did the sex itself. Which led to a question he wanted to ask but didn't know how to broach the subject. Now, with the pleasant glow settling around them and her soft breath falling across his chest, seemed like as good a time as any. "You've been putting off your apartment search until you have your first paycheck."

"Is this your not-so-subtle way of telling me to look faster, so I'm not living so far away?"

"Yes… and no." One thing he dreaded about the end of this trip—spending nights alone.

She looked up at him.

"My new place is big. Lots of bedrooms," he said.

A frown crept onto her face.

"And one is yours if you're interested."

Her frown deepened.

"Though, I hope if I earned my keep tonight, it'll be my room."

"Then where will you sleep?" Teasing danced on her face.

"If I'm lucky, in the same room as you. I don't like that you go home to a different place than I do. This trip spoiled me. Move in with me?"

She twisted her mouth. "I don't know… I might cramp your style. If I'm there, how are you supposed to engage in all that kinky debauchery you're so famous for?"

"I won't. I'll watch you do it. I'm really more of a voyeur."

"In that case, yes."

It was amazing how a single word could send so much joy through him. "That's your qualifier? If there's no nastiness, the deal is off?"

"If there's no sex stuff, I know you've been replaced by a pod person, and then yes, the deal is off." She slid from filthy talk back to innocence so easily, it almost made him hard again.

"As long as you're there, I want to be," Andrew said.

She cuddled against him, and they turned on the TV, to let a random show play in the background.

Her phone buzzed with a new message, and she ignored it.

He nudged her, hating to break up the mood but knowing it was necessary. "Shouldn't you make sure your sister knows you're alive?"

"I messaged her when we got in." Susan reached for her phone anyway. She sat straight up, scowling as she stared at the screen. "It's an email from my father. He wants to have lunch with me. Talk. Apologize for what happened in the heat of the moment."

Every inch of Andrew screamed to tell her *don't do it*. He swallowed urge. "How do you want to handle it?"

TWENTY-SEVEN

SUSAN CHECKED HER REFLECTION FOR THE FIFTIETH time in the last few seconds. She'd fought the impulse to dress like she did while working for her father, left the suit and skirt hanging in the closet she shared with Andrew, and opted for nice jeans and a T-shirt instead. The goal was to walk the line between being respectful and not bowing to her father's whims before she walked through the restaurant door.

She steeled herself and headed into Kandace's living room. The woman was a saint for letting them crash at her house, but Andrew would close on his soon. They'd only been back from their road trip a couple of days, so Susan hadn't imposed for too long. Lucas and Andrew were playing a card game. She loved that they were warming up to each other, and the way it made Andrew smile.

She watched for a few moments, letting the normalcy of the scene chase away her apprehension. When the nervous twitching moved back in, she straightened. "We should get going." They didn't have to be there for an hour, but she didn't want to be late. That, and there was no way she could sit still anymore.

Andrew didn't question it. He took her hand as they walked to her car. He' offered to drive, and she said *yes*, but the car was symbolic to her. Her father probably wouldn't see it, but she liked what it meant —that she didn't owe him anything.

As they headed up the canyon, her stomach tied itself into more and more knots, while she replayed snippets of her last conversation with the man—the things he said, how close she came to giving up her dream. Bile rose in her throat, carried on memories of him sabotaging the job she wanted. One she earned.

They walked into the restaurant, and though they were twenty minutes early, her father already waited at a table. He scowled when he saw Andrew.

Susan was more grateful than she thought possible for the reassuring arm Andrew wrapped around her waist as they approached the table. "Dad." She didn't bother to fake a smile. "You already know my boyfriend." She liked the way that tasted, rolling off her tongue.

Her father gestured to the chairs across from

him. "When you said, *we'll be there*, I thought you meant yourself and Melissa."

"If you want to break bread with Mercy, I won't be your buffer zone." She sat when Andrew held out her chair, then he took the spot next to her. "We can't stay long, but it looks like you weren't waiting for us anyway." She hid her wince at the passive-aggressive comment. If she was going to do this, she had to be direct. Part of her wished Andrew would step in. Take control of the conversation, rather than offer his support through a string of subtle touches and hand squeezes. She was grateful he kept quiet, though. If he spoke up, she wouldn't find the resolution she needed.

"How have you been?" Dad asked.

"Fine. I start teaching next week." It felt good to say that.

"May I ask where?"

"No."

A flicker of surprise crossed her father's face, before returning to normal. He cleared his throat. "I'll cut to the point and hope that alleviates some of this unneeded tension. The last time we spoke, a lot of things came out that shouldn't have."

She didn't like his phrasing. He left his comments open to misinterpretation. She'd let slide the implication that he was sorry he got caught, not that he felt that way to begin with. She'd prefer that they find some kind of tentative middle ground and work from there'. He was her dad, and she loved him despite everything. "I'm listening."

"I missed having you there for Christmas, and so did your brothers and sister."

That explained the Christmas afternoon message, but not the several-day lag till he emailed her. There was no reason to call him on the lie about her siblings.

"Funny, how it wasn't hard to find her when you put some effort into it," Andrew said.

She struggled to hide her grateful smile, especially when Dad scowled.

Andrew shrugged.

Her dad kept his attention on her. "I want you there for future holidays. What will it take, to make amends? I haven't stopped your school payments yet. I have your car when you're ready to take it back. Your phone needs an upgrade, though. We'll get you a new one."

"An apology would be a nice start." She swallowed her resentment at the realization he thought he could buy resolution. Bribe her to forget.

"I'm sorry you're not in our lives."

She gritted her teeth. "An apology for the cruel things you said."

"You mean the truth? Honesty isn't always pretty, hon. You're young, and you're rebelling. In five years or two, you'll thank me for saving you from the stupidity of youth."

ANDREW GROWLED at the string of thinly veiled insults and condescension. It took more restraint than he thought he had not to leap into the conversation.

Susan said, "You're right. I will."

Andrew clenched his jaw until it throbbed.

"So you'll stop all of this ridiculousness?" Dean asked.

Andrew couldn't sit through this. He opened his mouth, but Susan squeezed his knee. She met his gaze, and he bit back his scathing words.

She turned back to her father. "I will." The quaver was gone from her voice. The timidness that moved in the moment they walked into the restaurant was replaced with a thread of strength. "As of right now, I'm done pretending that I'm willing to rearrange my life for your approval. That you expect me to? That's some serious bullshit right there."

"Susan—"

"I don't want to sever ties." She cut Dean off. "You're welcome to be a part of my life, but only under my terms. *Accepting*—not tolerating, not making snide, back-handed comments—my career path and the man I love. That's all part of the *me* package."

Andrew couldn't hide his smug smile.

"You're being ridiculous," Dean said.

"Do you think so?" There was no hesitation in Susan's words.

"I do."

Susan stood, and Andrew was happy to join her. "Goodbye, Daddy. You know to find me if you grow up."

"Susan"—Dean's voice held a sharp edge—"if you walk out that door, you'll never touch my family again. Not my money and not my name. How long will the novelty of a rich, sleazy boyfriend make up for that?"

Andrew intertwined his fingers with hers and looked at Dean. "For as long as she'll have me." He hoped that was forever. Each time he looked at Susan, his love, admiration, and respect for her grew more.

He felt the tremor running through her as they walked away. He couldn't imagine how hard this was for her, but he was grateful she took this stand, rather than surrender herself to someone else's will.

One Month Later

Susan cycled through her stretches, to keep her muscles warm and limber. Around her, nearly two hundred other dancers did the same. The scents of makeup, sweat, and canvas felt natural, combined with the bright lights and polished floor.

It felt odd, filling out the application using the last name she'd had all her life. *Rice* didn't belong to her anymore, but she needed a replacement before she could ask people to call her anything else. She tried out *Rowe*, on Mercy's suggestion, but it didn't feel like it belonged to Susan.

She smiled and chatted with the people she recognized. Introduced herself to those who were new. Did everything she could, to distract herself from the nervousness churning inside.

The stress never left, regardless of the number of auditions she attended. It felt different this time, though. The gazes on her weren't as unnerving. Her biggest fear was how good the women around her were, and that was some hard-core competition.

Three dancers stepped to the front of the room, and a hush descended. It was an eerie kind of reverence. Susan paid attention to their every word. It didn't matter how many times she'd heard the *this is how it works* speech; she didn't want to miss anything.

The basics were simple. Each of the women up front would explain the dance she was looking to fill. The auditioning dancers would pick the one they were interested in, and the room would split into three groups. Once Susan made her choice, she and seventy-five or so others would learn the basics of their performance, and then show the evaluator, as a group.

Susan chose, and for the first time since she started attending try-outs, she ensured she was in the front row. The next few hours were a test of endurance and skill. She memorized the moves, let the music bleed into her until she knew the beat without hearing it, and flowed through the chore-ography.

She narrowed her focus, until the only things in her world were the vast parquet floor and the steps she needed to execute. She forced herself not to care who was watching.

Then, like that, it was over.

"Thank you, everyone, for attending. We'll be in touch with each of you within the next few days."

Like a switch had been flipped, the chatter burst back full-volume—girls talking about how they did, which moves were hardest, and *Oh my God, I hope I get this*.

She joined in, unable to wipe the smile from her face. This was normal too. After freezing the expression on during the audition, it would take time for her cheeks to relax. However, today it would stick around longer. She did well. There was no doubt. It might not be enough, but she'd never given a better performance.

She grabbed her bag, plucked her cell phone from it, and sent Andrew a text. *I'm done. Lunch?* Not that she'd be able to eat right away. The nerves clenching her stomach would calm as the day wore on.

His response didn't take long. *Duh? How'd it go? Hurry and get here, and I'll tell you.*

They were settling into a routine she loved. Andrew worked from home and had an open-door-at-the-house, knock-first-for-the-office policy with Lucas, who spent about half his afternoons there.

Susan kept busy with school—both teaching and attending. She was pretty sure the goofy grin she wore around Andrew would never fade.

We're outside. Where are you? he asked.

Yup. There was that grin. Most of the girls exited through the back and side doors, heading toward the parking. Susan took a guess and headed for the front of the building instead.

"Susan, do you have a minute?" Grace's familiar voice halted her.

Susan spun to face the director. Echoes of their last conversation tapped in her head. She blocked them out. She understood Grace's reasons for not offering her the job, but that didn't mean she liked them. There was also a risk she'd run into the same wall here, but she hoped to avoid it. "Sure. What can I do for you?"

"I saw part of your try-out. You're amazing," Grace said. "I'll be honest. I don't see dancers make this kind of turn-around very often."

"Thank you. I have a fantastic teacher."

Grace raised her brows. "Oh? Someone in the industry? Anyone I'd know?"

Susan swallowed a laugh. "In *an* industry, and if you've heard of him, you probably wouldn't admit it in polite company."

"Okay... The thing is there's still the issue we discussed last time."

"With Mr. Rice. Of course." Susan kept her tone pleasant, despite the curses streaming inside. "I was hoping you could make this decision based on my skill, rather than his checkbook."

"That's not quite fair."

Susan wasn't interested in turning this into a guilt-trip. She expected her father's money might come up and had a response. "Not to either of us. How about this? If you think I'm qualified—if his donation is the only thing holding you back—I'll raise whatever financial support he pulls if he makes good on his threat. Put me on the phones. Plant me in the middle of pledge drives. I'll do whatever it takes."

Andrew had offered to make up any donation needed. Susan told him the company could use the funding if he wanted to support them, but she wouldn't use it as leverage. She refused to bribe her way into a job—even one she'd been blackmailed out of.

Susan tried not to hold her breath while Grace chewed the inside of her cheek, her brow furrowed.

"You're right. I need to get input from everyone who led the auditions today, but I want you here. If you don't hear from me by the end of the week, call me," Grace said.

"I will. Thank you." Susan held back a squeal. It was too early to celebrate, but that didn't stop the party from kicking off in her brain. They said their goodbyes, and Grace disappeared back into the recesses of the building.

Despite the ample lighting in the studio, when Susan pushed outside, the glare of sun on concrete and snow made her blink several times until she adjusted.

"Hey, sexy. I was worried you changed your mind." A pair of arms wrapped around her waist, and Andrew kissed the back of her neck.

She leaned into him. "No you weren't. I bet you were too busy enjoying the view."

"Nope. Kept my eyes closed the entire time. Made it hard to walk, but I have a good guide."

"Hello." Lucas waved. He stood a few feet away.

Susan returned the gesture. "In that case, I'm sorry I kept you waiting."

Andrew squeezed her tight, before letting to go grab her hand. "You can make it up to me later."

Lucas stuck his fingers in his ears. "It's rude to talk about sex stuff. LALALALALA."

Susan laughed, and Andrew rolled his eyes before tugging Lucas's arms down. "We're behaving," Andrew said. "How'd it go?"

Susan related the conversation, not able to keep the anticipation from her voice. "I think I'm in. I *hope* I am."

"Never doubted you for a second." Andrew kissed her.

Lucas screwed up his face, then pulled at Susan's free hand. "Come on." He almost dragged her down the street. "We're going for ice cream."

She wasn't used to seeing this level of enthusiasm from him. Who was she to argue?

When they got to the ice-cream store, Lucas rushed to the counter. "One scoop of mint chocolate chip in a cone, please." He turned and looked at them. "*Hurry.*"

"What's up with the enthusiasm?" Susan asked.

Andrew shrugged. "Ice cream. Who needs a better reason?"

"Got it." She studied him. She couldn't figure out what was wrong with the scene. She placed her order, watching Lucas fidget the whole time.

He claimed them a table but sat at the edge of his seat, ignoring the sweet in his hand.

Andrew sat next to him and nudged him. "Hey. Calm down. You can go."

Lucas sat straighter and looked at Susan. "I know you're hesitating about changing your last name, and I get that, because you've had the old one for a long time."

She fought a smirk at the scripted language so very unlike the boy.

He was doing a good job of reciting the words. He went on. "The thing is we have a perfectly good last name, if you'd like to use it."

Andrew slipped him a twenty-dollar bill. "Perfect."

Lucas's meaning spread through her, carried on a warm glow, and she couldn't fight her grin. She looked at Lucas. "Did he bribe you to propose to me?"

Lucas nodded and dove into his ice cream.

"Women love children and perverts. Isn't that how the saying goes?" Andrew said.

Susan laughed. "It's children and dogs."

"That's what I said." He slid from his chair and dropped to one knee in front of her. "Here's the serious bit, in case you were wondering. I love you dearly and completely, Susan. I want you in my life until we're old and gray and then some, but only if Lucas is okay with it. Lucky me, that worked out. So, most honest-to-God genuine and sincere thing I've ever said—I want to marry you, if you'll have me. Will you be my wife?"

She leaned forward and kissed him, memorizing everything about the moment. The soft crush of his lips on hers. The texture of his tongue. The fine lines on his face under her fingertips, and the intoxicating sound of his low growl when he kissed back. Chatter in the background, squeals and laughter mingling with the scent of dozens of flavors of ice cream.

She sealed it all into a living image in her mind, and pulled back to look Andrew in the eye. There were few things she ever remembered wanting this much, and he'd helped her find all of them. "Yes. From now until forever, yes."

THANK you for reading Andrew and Susan's story.

If you'd like to meet more of Andrew and Mercy's friends, including discovering what the sexy, tattooed Justin gets up to, check out THEIR NERD. Antonio wants Justin, Justin wants Emily, and Emily wouldn't mind both of the above. Giving in could cost them everything.

- Grab your copy of THEIR NERD Today

TO READ Kandace's happily ever after, check out THE EXCEPTION. Kandace has spent her entire life making sure her family has what they need.

After a scorching one night stand in Italy, with a former TV star, she can't get the man out of her mind. When she meets the perfect man back home, where he's writing for her brother's newest film, she's swept off her feet again.

Then it turns out they have a past... with each other. They're also more than a decade younger than her. But the three can't ignore the sparks when they're together. Does Kandace dare make an exception to a lifetime of doing what's expected of her, or will she miss out on a chance at her own happily ever after... Twice?

- Check out **THE EXCEPTION** today